BETRAYED BY THE *L* WORD

BETRAYED BY THE L WORD | BOOK ONE

DAPHNE KANE

CONTENTS

To my amazing family.

This book probably wouldn't exist without all of your support

I love you.

AUTHOR'S NOTE

Please be aware that content in this story might include graphic references to topics such as sexual abuse.

CHAPTER ONE

August 9th, 2013

Sam

"Ow, Lance!" I'm startled awake, feeling my husband's teeth sinking into my labia.

Taking a minute to orient myself, I sit up slightly on my elbows, looking down to see my husband's head buried between my thighs.

"Sorry, baby," comes his deep reply. "You just taste so damn good," he pauses to place soft kisses on the insides of my thighs.

"When I got into bed and found you smelling this good, I couldn't help myself. I had to wake you in some kind of way. "He pauses once more to place more of those sinful kisses, causing my body to shutter. "I'm horny as hell, baby. I need my wife. Here, let me kiss it and make it better."

I willed myself to relax and settled back into my pillow, allowing him to do just that. Moments later, I feel my body heating as he starts his sinfully slow journey up. A soft moan escapes my lips when I feel his large hand clamp onto my breast before quickly sucking my nipple deep into his mouth. He gently laps at one nipple while punishing the other with a sharp pinch between his fingers. He adds just enough pain to balance all the pleasure that's starting to ripple through me. By the time his handsome face makes its debut, I'm panting and ready for more. Opening my legs wide to accommodate his large frame, I can feel his skillful fingers priming my slick opening for his entry. "Green-light, baby?" he murmurs into my ear, sending chills down my spine. A smile plays on my lips as I nod my head. That was all the confirmation he needed before plunging deep inside me.

An hour later, feeling my heart rate begin to slow and return to normal, I rolled over and snuggled up next to him. With a yawn, my eyes start to close as I feel sleep pulling me under.

"You know, baby, this would be a good time for you to go downstairs and work out." He whispers into my ear. ``I've already warmed you up. All you gotta do is go put in the work."

Not quite comprehending what he's suggesting, I glance at the clock on the nightstand and blink a few times to see it says 4:43 AM. *he has got to be joking*

"Lance..." I try saying before he cuts me off.

"Listen, Sam," he yawns before continuing. "I don't have a problem with it, I really don't, but you have to be more serious and committed about losing this weight." He's quiet for a minute before he releases a rough sigh. "Look, at your age, you have to work harder to see results. It is what it is, but you made a promise to me that you would make it happen. So what, are you going back on that promise now?"

I begin to feel the post-lovemaking bliss slowly leave my body. I briefly close my eyes before staring up at the sightless ceiling. "No, Lance," was my low reply as I slipped out of our bed and headed to the bathroom to get ready.

Taking in deep breaths, I lean forward, resting my hands on my kneecaps. After a few minutes, I've recovered enough to slowly make my way over to the small refrigerator in the corner. That forty-five-minute interval workout was brutal, and I'm contemplating if I even want to do the last twenty minutes on the treadmill. Just thinking about it has me glancing over, giving it the evil eye. I brought the water bottle to my lips, instantly groaning my satisfaction as the cold water cools me from the inside. I don't stop drinking until the bottle is empty. Wiping my sweaty face with my shirt, my mind wanders back to my childhood. Just how difficult it was growing up in a house with three skinny women. My twin sisters Eboni and Emoni, took after our mother. They were slim, petite, and ultra-beautiful. On the other hand, I had taken after my paternal grandmother, with my curvaceous plus-size frame, to my mother's dismay. We all have our mother's hazel eyes, warm cinnamon brown skin, and thick curly hair. With all the things I've accomplished in my life, my weight overshadows all of them in my mother's eyes. Taking a cleansing breath, I shake my head of those pesky thoughts and head over to the dreaded treadmill to finish this last twenty before heading back upstairs.

CHAPTER TWO

Sam

Standing in the shower, I close my eyes and let the warm water soothe my aching body. Grabbing my favorite pink pomegranate body wash, I inhale the delicious fruity smell as I begin to lather. I often daydream about taking long showers with Lance in this beautiful bathroom. It is a gorgeous space. I turn around, taking in the gorgeous mosaic tile throughout the bathroom. We spared no expense designing our "dream bed and bathroom." I wanted to walk through the double doors and feel like I'd stepped into a hideaway villa in Fiji. But sadly, I could never feel comfortable enough taking off all of my clothes in front of him. Especially not right now with this added weight I'm carrying, "No, ma'am, not gonna happen." I say out loud, releasing a sad chuckle.

I always try to keep things sexy, for him, with semi-see-through gowns or negligées. I make sure to always be slightly covered. I know it's insane, Lance is my husband, not just some new boyfriend. I know he does love me. He just kinda would prefer that I was a bit smaller. He constantly sends me articles on anti-aging and losing weight over forty. I know he's doing it to help me, but I don't think he realizes how much it's hurting me. Releasing the air I was holding in my lungs, I squeezed my eyes shut. I just want to make him happy. My mother often tells me, I'm fortunate to have such a successful and handsome husband my size. Maybe she's right.

With my heart weighing heavily inside my chest, I give my head a shake, trying to redirect my thoughts. *"Stop it, Samantha, stop that shit right now."* Deciding to let it all go for now, I tilt my head back and let the warm water rain down on my face. My mind quickly goes over all the things I plan to do today. I'm meeting up with Shell to do some shopping. I also want to check in on Ms. Sadie, my spunky eighty-eight-year-old neighbor. Just thinking about her puts a smile on my face. Two things you can count on getting from Ms. Sadie—a good laugh and a ton of gossip. She is extremely nosey and somehow knows everybody's business.

I still don't know how she's able to find out all the small details she's able to share. She also seems to be a bit of a fortune-teller, from knowing who's pregnant to who will be divorcing. She also proudly shares whose marriage will last a lifetime like her own. When I asked her about my and Lance's marriage, I noticed she would always politely change the subject or somehow get out of answering my question. It always leaves me with an uneasy feeling in the pit of my stomach, so I stopped asking. I always feel the need to check in on her since she lives alone now—by choice—of course. After her husband died, she turned down all four of her children's offers to live with them, to their dismay. They all knew there was no point in arguing with her; once her mind was made up about something, that was that. I have a pretty good relationship with all of her children, and I let them know I didn't mind checking in on her from time to time, being it's something I've been doing for the past four years now anyway. I simply adore her.

While I stood in front of the large mirror in my closet, I took in my reflection. I chose a deep purple maxi dress with large kimono sleeves. I paired it with gold sandals, and jewelry to finish the look. Being a plus-size woman, I have to be mindful of what I wear, something Lance is always quick to remind me. Yesterday, I took the time to wash, deep condition, and twist my hair. I'm rewarded with a big beautiful twist out, I'm currently finger combing. My husband is not a huge fan of my natural hairstyles, but there's not much I can do about that today. My hair appointment isn't for another two days, so he's just going to have to deal with it; plus, I actually like rocking my natural hair. *Sam, you're so pretty for a big girl* I can hear my mother say in my head as I use my pinky to make sure no lipstick is out of place. My hand stills as I close my eyes, and my head drops back. "Why…Why do I allow this woman to live rent-free in my head?" I ask out loud. Stepping back, a sigh leaves my lips, which ends in a little laugh. I turn and head downstairs.

"Killa? Where's my baby at?" I yell while listening out for him. Knowing I wouldn't have to wait for very long, my miniature gray French bulldog comes tearing around the corner. "There he is!" I say with excitement as he crashes into the hem of my dress, causing me to laugh. "Are you ready to go outside and handle some business?" I ask, looking down at him. He does his adorable three little twirls to let me know he is. I grab his leash off the table, and we head outside.

CHAPTER THREE

August 10, 2013

Lance

As I'm drinking my coffee, I watch Sam from the kitchen window. Killa has me laughing out there, trying to chase a squirrel bigger than him. "All right, big man, I've already warned you about messing with those squirrels. One day, they're going to take you up on what you're offering." I murmur, taking a sip of coffee. Feeling my cell phone vibrate, I glance down at the screen and smile. Bringing the phone to my ear, I ask, "Gio, what's good?" to my best friend.

"Nothing much, my brotha," he replied in that thick Italian accent of his. Gio is my brother from another mother. We've been friends since college. With my dark brown skin and his olive skin tone showcasing his Italian heritage, we were definitely a hit with the ladies. Hell, we still are.

With my eyes still tracking Sam, I tell him, "Man, you should see Sam out here walking Killa. It's some funny shit."

"Let me guess. She's out there looking like a plus-size supermodel, with a poop bag in her hand, as Killa's less than nothing ass drags her down the street." He finishes laughing.

His description of my wife has me cracking up. "I don't know about the supermodel part just yet, but we're going to get her there." I laugh.

"What are you two getting into on this fine Saturday?" Gio asks.

"I would invite you over, but... I was recently informed that we have a green light situation, so…"I finish while rubbing my hands together.

"Well, may the force be with you."

"What?! Gio, what in the hell does that even mean?" I shake my head, laughing at another one of my friends' crazy sayings.

"Just remember, you're not a spring chicken anymore, is all I'm saying. I wouldn't want you pulling a hammy, so pace yourself," he chuckles into the phone.

After a while, I notice that he's gone quiet. "Hey man, are you still there?" I ask, looking at the phone to make sure the call hasn't dropped.

"Can I ask you something?" Comes his somber reply.

"Uh oh, what's on your mind, man?" I ask him, leaning back against the counter.

"Have you ever thought about telling her?"

Confused for a second, I ask, "Tell who what?"

When he remained silent for a little too long, I knew exactly who he was speaking of.

"COME ON, MAN," I'm instantly seeing red as I slam my coffee mug on the counter. "Maybe if you had kept some shit to yourself for once, you'd still be married, so stop speaking on me and mine."

I knew it was a low blow as soon as the last word left my lips. Gio had become the sole provider for his aging parents not too long after he and Corinne were married. Knowing his wife would have a problem with it, he chose to keep it from her. One day, with his guilt riding him, he broke down and told her the truth. Being the gold digger I knew her to be, she was mad as hell, but what I didn't expect was for her to pack up and leave him after five years of marriage. Gio treated that woman like a queen. That was an asshole move of me to throw that into my friend's face so callously.

As I hang my head, I tell him, "I'm sorry, man, that was uncalled for."

"No, I need to stay in my lane. It's just that I've known Sam for a long time, and I don't want to see her hurt."

"I know, man, I know," I say, as a burst of air leaves my lips. "Don't worry, I'm dealing with it, and have it under control."

"Ok, but if you need to talk, I'm here, no judgment," was Gio's reply.

"On a lighter note, next Saturday is Sam's birthday."

"That's right!" was Gio's excited reply, "I'm just shocked she agreed to a pool party. You must have put LJ up to it," he laughs. "Wait a minute, next Saturday? Isn't that the weekend we fly out to Austin, Texas, to start the layout for the new Musk headquarters? Damn man, Is Sam upset we'll be leaving her party early?" He finishes with concern coating his words.

"Naw, she's cool. She actually finished finalizing all of our reservations yesterday. If anybody understands business, it's Samantha Lane, but, to be on the safe side, you should probably think about bringing her a bottle of tequila. Make sure that shit is rare and...

"Expensive as hell," Gio finishes for me."

"Exactly." I laugh.

"How many bottles of tequila does she have now? She's been collecting them since college."

"Man, I couldn't tell you, but if a bottle is so much as facing a different direction, she will go "Kathy Bates in Misery on you." Thinking about my ambitious wife, I sober up before saying, "I have to watch her, though; she's been talking more and more about having her own tequila brand. She's even talking about opening a tequila distillery or some shit."

"What's wrong with that? You don't think that's a good idea? You can't deny, the woman knows her shit about tequila and business," Gio chuckles.

"I know, I just think her focus needs to be more on home, on me, you know what I'm saying. She should just let me take care of her. Plus, she's pushing forty-five; why would she want to compete with people/women half her age? There's not much she can do about getting older, but maybe she would have a fighting chance if she worked a little harder at losing some weight."

Gio lets out a low whistle before saying

"That's harsh, man. I'm hoping you've never said anything remotely like that to your wife. Sam's brilliant. That woman could start a successful business with her eyes closed, and you know it. GLS wouldn't be as nearly as successful if not for Sam's business savvy. The best thing we could have ever done was bring her on board to start this business back in college. I know that's your wife, and you love her dearly, but man, give that woman her flowers.

Sam

As I walked up, overhearing Lance saying those words gutted me. I know my age, and I know what I look like. I have a battle in my head daily about being too old or too fat, just undesirable to my husband. Most days, I win the battle, but, from time to time, my mind wins. With a sigh, I plaster a smile on my face as I enter the kitchen. A surprised look covers Lance's face.

"Baby, look..."

I held my hand up to stop him from apologizing. He was just being honest, I can't fault him for that, even if it hurts like hell.

"Is that Gio? Hey, Gio!" I say into the phone. I kiss my husband's speechless lips before grabbing my purse and keys. "I'm about to meet up with Shell to do some shopping for the party. I won't be gone long," I wink at him and head to the garage.

Once inside my car, I release a shaky sigh and lean my head against the steering wheel. I know Lance is right. I have a good life. Maybe I should just worry about being a good wife and consider myself lucky.

"Let's go, Sam; you do not have time for this," I whisper to myself. I took a cleansing breath, started my car, and pulled out of the driveway.

While driving down the street in silence, I allow myself to bask in this beautiful Northern California morning. Glancing up, I see the beautiful rosy hues the sun has cast across the sky. I've lived in the San Francisco Bay Area my entire life. I will be the first one to say, I've been spoiled by the wonderful weather we have almost all year around. I never take for granted the beautiful sunrises and sunsets that give me so much peace as I watch them color the sky. I love to watch the beautiful morning sky. It will never get old. Feeling better, I decided I wanted to surprise my bestie with some coffee. I turn left at the light to head in the direction of our favorite coffee spot.

CHAPTER FOUR

Shell

While looking for swimsuits, Shell notices how quiet Sam has been for the past thirty minutes. She turns to watch as Sam vaguely pays attention to the bathing suits she's looking at as Sam absently sips her coffee.

"What's up, Sam?" I whisper, trying to get her attention. My first thought was maybe she was a bit self-conscious about trying on bathing suits. Looking deeper into those beautiful hazel eyes, I can see sadness lurking. Instantly on high alert. I yell, "Who fucking with you?" causing the few women in the shop to turn and stare.

"Shell!" Sam quietly reprimands me.

Anyone that knows me, Michelle (Shell) Johnson knows there are two people in this world I do not play about—my little sister Cassie and my bestie Samantha. They're the only two people that truly give a shit if I'm dead or alive. There's nothing I wouldn't do for either one of them. A bit softer, I ask, "Who fucking with you, Sam?"

She laughs at my restraint and tells me what she overheard Lance saying.

I closed my eyes and took a cleansing breath before beginning. "Sammy, why do you do this to yourself? We're in our forties, SO FUCKING WHAT? I'm still that bad bitch I've always been. I own an extremely successful real estate brokerage firm and have a plethora of good dick at the ready. And you, my gorgeous friend, are part owners of one of the most successful commercial construction firms in the country! Oh! and let's not forget about those big titties and juicy ass that I'm so jealous of." She says with a wink. "Out here having these men losing their minds. Everywhere we go, you're catching some man's eye. Lance knows what he has and knows exactly what he's doing. That's why his ass holds on so tight."

I stopped my rant for a second to grab her hands before continuing. "But, girly, you have to start seeing your worth for yourself. If you want your tequila brand, then go get it! Hell, you want to own your agave field to make the damn tequila, then go get that shit too. I'm not quite sure how it all works, but I know if anyone can figure it out, it's Samantha Victoria Lane. So stop letting your insecurities get in your way, fuck how anyone else sees you. All that matters is how you see your damn self." As I finish my rant, I lean over, bumping my shoulder into hers.

Sam finally smiles, then I smile. Next thing, we're cracking up. Pulling her in for a tight hug, a scary thought crosses my mind, if my friend doesn't see that she's beautiful inside and out, or face her fears, I'm afraid she's going to allow all her hopes and dreams to pass her by, and that's the last thing I want for my dearest friend.

CHAPTER FIVE

Sam

After a couple of hours of trying on bathing suits, Shell and I walk out laughing, each carrying multiple bags. "I just find it hard to believe that all of the bathing suits I picked out for myself were out of stock, but every single one you picked out for me they had." I glare at her before continuing. "If I find out you paid those poor women to deceive me, I'm going to get you, Shell. Now I'm stuck with this way too revealing swimsuit ensemble, Lance is going to have a fit."

"Girl, stop. You looked gorgeous in that swimsuit, and you got the coverup to go with it. Your body is practically hidden," she says, making sure to keep her eyes averted.

I start to laugh as I call my best friend out on her lie. "Michelle Marcella Johnson, are you going to stand there and tell me that bald-faced lie? You know that mesh cover-up isn't covering anything." I continued to chuckle as I watched her.

With a guilty look, she says, "I know, I know, Sam. I'm lying through my damn teeth, but that's because you looked gorgeous in that outfit." She averts her eyes once again before saying, "and yes, maybe I did slip the sales lady a one-hundred-dollar bill to hide those atrocious swimsuits you wanted to try on." She says unapologetically.

I roll my eyes as she continues.

"I need you to know there's nothing wrong with showcasing what you have while also reminding Lance what he has."

Under her breath, I hear her say, "And anyway fuck him."

I ignore her sly remark, and I hesitantly ask, "So… are you planning on bringing anyone special to my party?" I keep my eyes on her to make sure she doesn't throw anything at me.

"Now, why would I want to do some stupid shit like that, Samantha?" She says with her hands on her hips.

I try my best not to laugh or enrage her anymore and give her an innocent look before saying, "I was just thinking maybe you could invite Rodney?" I finish in a small voice, knowing she's about to blow up.

"See, bitch, this that shit I am talking about," she says, pointing her finger at me.

I can only laugh when Shell gets like this. No matter how successful she is or how many awards and accolades line her walls, come at her crazy, and she will gladly remind you she's from Watts, California and does not have a problem clearing all this shit out—her words.

"Shell, listen, sweetie," I calmly say to her, "you are always there for me and have always had my back, I need for you to know, I've got yours too." Noticing she hasn't attacked me yet, I rush to finish. "Rodney adores you. He's successful, and let's not forget the man is fine as hell. Maybe you should give-" I stop instantly when I see her tilt her head.

"Samantha, I love you with everything that's in me, but if you were about to say I should give Rodney a chance, I'm sorry, but we can no longer be friends." She threatens with a challenging stare.

I looked into her eyes and tried to gauge how serious she

was. I decided not to test her and said, "Girl, I was only going to say, you should give Rodney his flowers. I mean, the brotha is fine and all." I finish on bated breath.

She watches me for what feels like forever before saying. "Girl, you ain't ever lied; he is fine, and the way the man handles my lady bits is transcendent. Hell, maybe I should give him a call," she says that last part almost to herself.

I turn to walk towards the car and let out a sigh of relief, thinking a crisis had been averted, until I hear...

"And you, bitch."

I groan, turning back to her, holding up my hands in surrender. "Look, I promise it won't happen again. I won't speak on Rodney matters unless you bring them up. Deal? I just want you to be happy, Shell. I love you, girl." I whine to her.

She comes over and hugs me. "I know you do, Sam, but I'm happy as long as my girls are happy, ok?" Pulling back, she looks into my eyes before saying, "Come on, girl, let's go get something to eat. My treat." hooking her arm in mine, we walk towards her black Tesla.

In the car, I think about something Shell said back there. Maybe Lance needs to be reminded of what he has. Even if I don't wholeheartedly believe that, come next Saturday, I'm planning to fake it until I make it.

CHAPTER SIX

Sam

After an uneventful weekend with Lance, shopping with Shell, and visiting with Ms. Sadie, I'm ready for the week. Especially with my first stop being LJ's shop. Just thinking about my boy has me hurrying to grab my things and, of course, my fur baby Killa before scurrying out the door. Once in the car, my cell rings. Digging through my purse to retrieve it, I let out a frustrated sigh once I see who's calling. Placing the phone to my ear, I say, "Good morning Adriana. How may I help you, dear?"

I can't for the life of me understand why Lance hired this girl to be his assistant. She has to call me for every damn thing, even after five months of working at GLS. I don't mind helping, I really don't, but at this point, it's downright annoying. She calls me for every little thing. *"Hi Sam, what do you think Lance would want me to order him for lunch?" Hi Sam, I'm in Starbucks. Does Lance prefer skim milk or cream again?"*

"Hi, Sam, I'm in Costco and forgot the food and supply list to

restock the breakroom. Could you please send it to me? This girl, I think, rolling my eyes.

"Thank you for answering, Sam. My mother slipped and fell in her bathroom this morning. She has a small bump on her head where she hit it on the sink. I'm going to take her to Kaiser this morning, so I won't be in today."

"Oh, no! I'm sorry to hear that. Go ahead and take the day. I will make sure Lance is covered."

'Thanks, Sam, you're the best!" She says before hanging up.

I rest my head against the steering wheel, breathing deeply while counting to ten. My heart aches, knowing I will have to cut my visit with my son short. LJ is my whole heart. Not only is he my only child, but he's also my best friend. I wanted more children, but Lance thought it best to have only one to ensure we both could succeed in our careers. He also said we could revisit the talk of having another baby after our careers took off. *"Let's just hold off on more kids right now. It's already like we have two babies with LJ and GLS. Let's stay focused, Sam. It's grind time!"* After LJ was born, we decided on the rhythm method to prevent pregnancy that Lance perfected. That man knows my periods better than I do to ensure I wouldn't get pregnant. Of course, that talk of more children never happened, and now I'm too old.

The thought of my son's handsome face makes me smile. I shake off my blues as I head over to see my pride and joy.

As I pull up to my baby boy's place of business, I'm instantly overcome with pride. Leaning forward to peek out the windshield, I look up to get a better view of the large orange sign on the front of the building that reads LL moving Co. Not only did LJ buy his first home (with Shell's Guidance) when he was twenty-three, but now at twenty-six, he owns a successful four-men moving company. Grabbing Killa and my purse, I eagerly step out of the car.

I place Killa down with his leash attached and open the back door to grab the bags and pan of food I brought with me. Stepping back from the car to close the door while juggling all the stuff in my hands presented more of a challenge than I anticipated. I knew I was in trouble once I felt my heel catch the back of my dress when I took a step back. "Oh no, oh no, oh no," I chant as I feel myself begin to fall. Suddenly, strong arms grab me from behind, blocking my fall. I look over my shoulder to see which one of the guys came to my rescue. Smiling up, I say, "thank you, Jay, you probably just saved my life. I hope I didn't hurt you." Then, instantly concerned about his safety, "I am too damn big to be this clumsy." I chastise myself.

"Naw, you're perfect Mrs. Lane." He says with a smile that reaches his beautiful eyes. Grabbing the pan out of my hands, he leads the way into the building.

I can't help but marvel at Jay's hair as I walk behind him. He's a beautiful mix of his African American mother and Hispanic father. With his medium brown skin and kind light brown eyes, his hair was the showstopper if you ask me. Silky jet black wavy hair, that he usually keeps up in a man bun. The few times I've caught it flowing down his back was truly a sight to behold. As he holds the door open for me, I go on and drop a hard truth on this young man.

"Now, Jay, this weekend is my birthday, and I will be treating everybody to shots of my favorite tequila. I do have to tell you this, my tequila has been known to knock grown men on their asses. I'm telling you this because I cannot be held responsible if you just so happen to wake up the next morning with a shaved head." I pause to let what I just said sink in. I clear my throat, trying to conceal my laughter as he throws me a look over his shoulder to gauge if I'm serious or not.

"You just saved my life out there. I thought it only right to warn you. Now, let's just say, a few weeks from now, if I just so happen to walk up in here with a new wig flowing down my back, I don't want you wondering if it's your hair, sweetie, because it most definitely will be. The moral to the story, don't let me catch you slipping at my party with that beautiful hair." He finally stops and turns back to look at me. I hold a straight face for as long as I can before cracking up. Laughing harder as I look up at his confused expression, I finish by telling him he has gorgeous hair.

LJ's laugh reaches my ears as he steps out of his office. "You know she's playing, right?"

"Or, is she?" I say, turning my face into stone once more.

"Yeah, I know she is," Jay replied, smiling, showcasing his deep dimples.

"What's all this, Ma," LJ says, looking into the bags.

"I cooked way too much food over the weekend, I figured you fellas would like some, plus you know how your father is about fried food in the house."

"Yeah, I know," was his uninterested reply. "Is he still giving you a hard time about your weight?" He looks at me with a questioning stare.

"Come on, son, don't start.' I tell him, rubbing his arm.

"That beautiful voice can only come from one person." I heard someone say from behind me. Turning around, I see Mason and Cole headed our way. I laugh as I look up into this giant white boy's face. Mason is a hottie. He's big, blonde, and a straight badass. From his many piercings to his scattered tatts across his body, Mason screams bad boy for life, but I know his secret. He's a real gentleman that happens to be a mad flirt. Case in point, he leans his big body in to help me with the bags in my hands, but not before inhaling deeply and commenting on how good I smell. This leads to LJ telling him to knock it off. We all laugh, we know he's playing… well kind of.

"Hey Cole, how's it going?" I say as he approaches. Cole is a few years older than the other guys. I believe he just recently turned thirty-three. He's also a bit more reserved. He's putting his baby sister Jasmine through college, and I smile with pride.

He's more about his money than getting involved with office banter. I can only respect that. I love to see hard-working young men with ambition. Cole is also very easy on the eyes. Like the rest of the guys, my baby boy included. Cole has that whole Jesse Williams, Jeremy Meeks thing going on for him. Light skinned blue eyes, brotha with gorgeous thick pink lips. You know, if you happen to be into that sort of thing. Shell would definitely eat him up, I snort to myself.

"I'm sorry you didn't hear from me over the weekend, LJ. We kind of had a green light situation over at the house, so…" I trail off, smiling wickedly, knowing what's coming.

"Ma, please stop!" He says, bringing his hand up, trying to stop me from going further. "I don't want to hear about it. I won't come over, I'll just call for the next four-seven days. It's bad enough that I know why and how many days I need to stay away."

I laugh as my baby leans in to hug me.

Right as I'm about to head into LJ's office to have a seat and visit with him, Mason asks, "what's a green light situation?"

"Please, no!" LJ begs as a huge grin splits my face. Too late, LJ realizes it's too late. I set my purse back down and prop my hip against the desk, ready to educate.

I hear a deep sigh from my son, so I decide to take pity on him. "LJ, I'm an educator by nature, but I promise not to go too in-depth, deal? I ask expectantly. He looks up at me, smiling, letting me know I can proceed.

I turn back to the guys before saying, "As you all may know, Lance and I have only one child, and that was by choice. When we decided to close up shop, we talked to our doctor about various birth control options. I knew I wanted something easy and hormone-free. So that cut out birth control pills or an IUD, and we all know the pull-out method is just unreliable."

"MA!" LJ exclaims.

"Sorry, moving on," I say with my hands up. "When we came

across the rhythm method, we knew that was the one for us. It gave us complete control once we understood how it worked. The reason I'm sharing this with you is that if you haven't already, you will one day meet someone special. After quite some time, and you feel it's serious enough and going to be something long-term, I want you to make safe, effective decisions. I believe women are more aware of this method, but it couldn't hurt for guys to know how this works as well."

"In a nutshell, a woman is only fertile a certain number of days during the month. You learn when these fertile days are and abstain from sex or use condoms. These are the red light days. Some form of contraception is needed. Then, there are the non-fertile days, where no condom is needed. There are tons of apps available to help pinpoint these days." I raise my finger, pointing at all of them as I reiterate. "Only if you're in a committed relationship for quite some time, and you trust each other wholeheartedly. It's very important you fully understand these red and green days if you're going to attempt this method. Red light STOP, green light GO, you can fu-"

"MA, please!"

"Have sex," I glare at my son as I continue, "Like bunnies and know that no pregnancy with come of it. With that being said, using condoms is always a great choice. Now, are there any questions?" I look around, taking in the various degrees of discomfort on their faces. Rolling my eyes, I grab my purse as a frustrated burst of air leaves my lips.

"Come on, guys, we're all grown folks here," I tell them, creasing my forehead. "I'm only trying to arm you with alternative methods of birth control. But let me repeat this," I state with a finger high in the air, "only when you're in a committed relationship, this won't work with no slide. You make sure you strap up every single time. It may not feel as good, but…"

"Okay, Ma, they have to get back to work."

"Boy, did you just cut me off? You don't want to get me started on other topics, do you?" I ask pointedly.

"Ok, mama, I'm so sorry. I will do anything to spare them the talk on safer oral sex practices. I'm sorry." He says with both hands up. Taking pity on him, I chuckle under my breath, thinking my work here is done. I grab my purse and head into his office so we can catch up before I have to head to work.

~

LJ

After walking my mom to her car and seeing her off, I head into the breakroom to talk to the guys. "I'm sorry about that; she's only trying to help."

"I don't know why you're apologizing. You act like we're just meeting your mom," Mason says while going through the food. Looking up from the bags, he glanced behind him at the large clock on the wall before saying, "Plus, I'm going to say this now because, technically, we still have another fifteen minutes before we clock in, and you're my boss. Your mother is one of the sexiest women I know, man."

Before I have a chance to check his ass, Jay and Cole decide to take this opportunity to chime in. I guess because "technically," I'm not their boss either right now. I think sarcastically.

"There's just something about her, man," Cole says while shaking his head and looking down. "It's just.. the way she walks, talks, smells, just how she carries herself in general, is just captivating." I'm standing there with my arms crossed, shocked as shit, hearing this come from Cole, of all people. I want to get mad at all of them, but I understand. This is nothing new to me when it comes to my mom. She has that effect on men without even trying or even being aware that she's doing it —from my little league coaches to my college teammates. I believe it's her kind heart that pulls the opposite sex to her. I hope to marry someone just like her. How she loves my father, even though I don't believe he deserves her, has me looking forward to finding love like that one day. Of course, I don't say this to the guys. I want them to know I think it's really fucked up they can't keep themselves from lusting after my mother. It's just wrong. "I can't wait for one of y'all mothers to come in for a visit. I plan to give her the VIP treatment of LJ moving." Looking down at my watch, I sound off. "It's been fifteen minutes, now go clock your asses in and stop lusting after my mama! He turns and heads to his office with his employees laughing at his back.

What LJ doesn't see is that one of his men isn't laughing at all. His expression holds a look of a man in deep thought and determination.

CHAPTER SEVEN

Sam

I always have a blast hanging out with my son and his crew. They're a great bunch of guys. I can't help feeling motherly towards them all. After stopping at Starbucks and Lance's favorite vegan bakery, I'm finally pulling into the GLS construction parking lot. Sadness grips me so suddenly that my eyes water, distorting my vision. The great sense of pride I used to feel when I pulled up to this building is no longer there. I reminisce over the countless late-night cram sessions with Lance and Gio when we were trying to get this business off the ground. I was front and center with all aspects of the business. Over the years, as the business grew, and became more successful, my contributions became smaller and less crucial until I basically became Lance's secretary. I worked my ass off to earn my MBA. Laying my head back against the headrest, once again, my mother's voice floats through my mind. *That man wants a housewife, Samantha, so you be a housewife. You can't afford to be too picky, baby, I'm just saying.* Killa lets out a couple of barks, alerting me I've gone too quiet. I look back at him and smile. "Mama, fine baby, let's go get this day started.

Now sitting at my desk, with Killa chilling in his plush bed in the corner, I lean over to open my blinds and turn on my computer. Moments later, I'm so distracted going through emails, I don't hear Gio enter my office until I hear his deep voice.

"Good morning, my dearest Samantha? How are you this fine morning?"

I quickly glance up to see one of my oldest and dearest friends' handsome faces leaning against the door frame. I can't help but smile.

"Good morning, Giovanni! How was your weekend? I hope you didn't leave too many broken hearts scattered across the Bay Area." I joke, biting on the tip of my ink pen.

"Nope, not one broken heart left behind—well, not by me anyway. I spent the weekend with my parents in Napa… wine tasting," he drops off.

"Uh oh, how did Mr. Rossi enjoy that," I almost hate to ask, bringing my hands up to cover my smile?

With a sigh, Gio recounts how his seventy-four yr old Italian father harassed the poor people about how wrong they were going about preparing the wine. Gio only recently was able to convince his aging parents to move here from their beloved Italy. Let's just say it's been a huge adjustment for everyone.

I couldn't help laughing after he told me the whole story, so I decided to go give my friend a much-needed hug. I walked around my desk with my arms open, and Gio met me halfway for our embrace. I always feel so protected in his arms. Inhaling deeply, I allow his delicious scent to fill my nose. Pulling back, I gaze up into the greenest eyes I've ever seen. You have to be careful around Gio. His magnetic charm will draw you in every single time. He will have some poor unsuspecting woman ready to drop her panties on the spot with just a glance from that seductive gaze. I think, laughing at the thought. Looking up at him, I ask about his parents.

"They're wonderful. My mother asked about you," He says, smiling down at me.

"Oh, yeah? How is Mrs. Rossi? I was thinking maybe we could all go out to dinner one day soon. There's this Italian restaurant I found that had rave reviews. They supposedly serve the best and most authentic Italian food in the Bay Area. I don't know how true that is, but do you think your parents would be interested?"

"If you're there, most definitely. They both adore you as much as I do, Samantha." He says in that beautiful accent of his. *"See, way to smooth for his own good."*

Starting to feel bashful, I step out of his embrace and retreat to the safety of my desk.

Gio doesn't turn to leave my office as I expected, he surprises me by coming inside and sitting in the chair across from me.

I tilt my head to one side, and I ask. "Is there something else on your mind, Gio?"

As he clears his throat, he moves to the edge of his chair before looking straight into my eyes. "Look, Sam, I've always admired your tenacity and drive. No one knows more about tequila or business than you. You're a smart, vivacious woman who could hold her own in that male-dominated business if you chose to.

As he finishes his heartfelt statement, with green eyes glowing with determination, I do what I do best. I plaster a smile on my face and say the words I'm supposed to say.

"Thank you, Gio, for being a great friend and believing in me, but I'm truly content with my life right now. Plus, this isn't the time to disrupt things. GLS has been extremely busy with all the new accounts coming in."

Right when he's about to respond, I'm saved by the bell as the phone begins to ring.

"I will talk to you later," I whisper to him before answering the phone. "Thank you for calling GLS construction. You've reached Lance Lane's office. How may I help you?"

As I wave Gio goodbye, I notice he frowns at me before standing and walking away.

I know that was a cowardly move. I'm just not ready to talk about it. After finishing the call, I replaced the receiver and sighed. Leaning my head back, I'm momentarily filled with dread thinking about my birthday party this weekend. I know I will get through it as I do with everything else in my life. It just seems so daunting right now. Shaking off the last of my blues, I throw myself into my work for the rest of the day.

CHAPTER EIGHT

August 17, 2013

Sam

"You can do this. You can do this, Samantha." I chant to myself while taking in my reflection. "Why did I let that girl talk me into buying this scandalous bathing suit ensemble?" I say to no one. Not that it's super revealing I am practically covered from head to toe. The problem is, with all these curves, on my size eighteen body, there's not much I can do to hide them in this. I'm wearing a white see-through mesh dress that glides over my body before falling to my feet. It has two long slit-ups on each side. Beautiful vibrant colors make a swirl pattern around the dress. I remember telling Shell I would look like a big ass walking bag of jolly ranchers with all these colors. Underneath, I'm wearing a cream-colored halter one-piece bathing suit that can clearly be seen. I keep the jewelry simple with large thin gold hoop earrings and some gold bangles on my wrist. I look down at the gold sandals on my feet that make my marshmallow-colored toenails pop. I found a video on

YouTube that showed me how to make my twist-out last longer. My week-old twist-out is full and luscious today, absolutely perfect with this outfit.

I grab a Kleenex to wipe my sweaty hands before heading downstairs. Letting the loud music guide me to where the party was, I step into our large backyard as all my friends and family begin to cheer. Smiling at everyone, I immediately look through the crowd to locate my men. Spotting them lounging near the pool, I head in that direction. I'm momentarily distracted when I see Shell and Cassie coming into the back-yard from the side entrance. Of course, once Shell and I spot each other, it is over. As we're making our way to one another, I notice one of her breasts was dangerously close to popping out of that tiny white bikini she's rocking. Laughing, I adjust her top before we throw our arms around each other. Instantly, I feel a strong tug from behind as I'm pulled back. Confused, I glanced over my shoulder to see my husband glowering at me.

"Can you please control yourselves? You both are putting on a show for all the men here?" He growls into my ear. Taken completely off guard by his words, I'm left speechless. My hearing must have faded a bit because I finally begin to register Shell and Cassie, asking if I am alright.

Shell's gaze snaps up to Lance. "What in the hell did you say to her?"

"Back off, Shell, this is between my wife and me."

"No can do, buddy," she cuts him off, "it's her birthday," she points. "And I'm not allowing anyone to shit on it, not even you." She finishes with a smirk on her face and a challenge in her eyes.

Lance laughs as he takes a step back, running his hand over his mouth. "You know, I find that funny because, last I checked, this is my house, and I can do anything I damn well please."

"Is that so, Lance?" This comes from Cassie, Shell's little

sister, who was standing off to the side, shooting daggers at him with her eyes.

"You know what, I don't have time for this. I would like to speak to *my wife* privately, on her birthday. Excuse us."

Finally, coming out of my shock, I look up at my husband, hearing him say, "Can I talk to you, alone, please?" I snatch my hand from him as I walk past him towards our house. I may be mad at him and a little hurt by his actions, but what I'm not going to do is voice my displeasure with him in front of people. So he follows as I make my way back inside.

"What in the hell is wrong with you?" I turn and ask him as soon as we reach our bedroom. "You completely embarrassed me out there, Lance."

"I'm sorry, baby, I just... I was a little hurt." He says, "grabbing for my hand "I saw you were headed over to me and LJ when you first stepped outside, but once you spotted Shell and Cassie, you just forgot all about us, baby. I wanted to be the first to embrace the birthday girl, that's all." He finishes with a hurt expression.

I think over what he's saying to me. Putting my hand up to my temple while giving my head a little shake, I ask, "Ok, but what was with the hurtful comment about us putting on a show for the men? I just wanted to look and feel sexy for you, Lance."

"Baby, you don't have to do all this to look sexy to me." He says, looking me up and down. "You're my wife, and I adore you just as you are.

"Just as I am? What are you saying? Am I ugly or something?" I whisper to him, feeling my heart drop.

"No, baby," he says, grabbing me by my waist and looking down at me. "You're one of the most beautiful women I've ever met, and you're all mine. All I'm saying is, not everything's meant to be worn by everybody. Maybe you should have gone with something a bit more tasteful, something you already have in your closet."

I truly felt as if I'd been slapped. I stand there speechless and humiliated. My mind instantly goes to a time when I went shopping with my mother and sisters. I remember my mother's words. *"You have such a beautiful face, Sam, if only you'd lose some weight." "No, sweetie, you can't wear that. Your body type is all wrong to pull something like that off. We'll get this for one of your sisters and go find something more suitable for you." "Sam, if you don't put more effort into losing weight, you'll never find a husband."*

I refuse to entertain those kinds of thoughts, not today. I look damn good, and I know it. Not saying a word, I turn from my husband and I walk right out the door. I'm going to enjoy my forty-fifth birthday to the fullest. If anybody has a problem with that, they can kindly kiss my ass.

"Ma, you ok?"

LJ asks with worried eyes as he waits for me at the bottom of the stairs.

"Yes, Sonshine, I'm great!" I say, taking his hand.

"That's good to hear," he says, beginning to laugh.

Watching his shoulders begin to shake, I know something truly had him tickled.

"Boy, what's so damn funny?" I asked, getting annoyed.

As he tried to catch his breath, he finally said, "I knew dad would lose his shit once you stepped outside in this little number, Ma. Then when you went off course to greet Aunt Shell, instead of coming straight to him, I swear I saw steam coming out his ears. When you turned to Shell, giving everyone a glimpse of your backside..." LJ couldn't talk anymore. He was laughing so hard.

I'm beginning to feel more self-conscious by the second, *"maybe Lance was right about this outfit."*

LJ instantly sensed something was wrong. "Don't you dare do that, Ma. Do you know just how good you look, woman!" He asks, with excitement dancing in his eyes. "It's hilarious to me because dad needed to be reminded he's got himself a baddie, and this little get-up is definitely doing just that." He says, taking my hand and twirling me around, making me laugh at his antics. "He knows all eyes are on his beautiful wife. I knew he wouldn't handle this well. I figured he would probably try to say something hurtful to make you want to change your clothes," he finishes with disgust coating his words. "I'm so happy you didn't."

"You look amazing today, Ma. I'm most likely going to have to hire new employees because I'm pretty sure I'm going to have to fire my whole crew on Monday."

"Why do you say that, baby? You have an amazing crew."

He starts laughing again, taking in my puzzled expression. Pulling me in for a hug, he says, "I'm just playing. Happy birthday, mama."

"Thank you, baby," I say, feeling myself getting emotional.

"Come on, Sonshine, let's go have some fun!"

"Ok, I'll meet you out there. I'm going to the kitchen to get a few things. Did you need anything?"

"No, baby, go ahead. I will see you out back."

Once I step outside, the first thing I see is Cole staring at me from across the pool. He's lounging on one of the pool chairs, wearing swim shorts with a matching shirt that's opened down the front. He has his tattooed body on full display today. As I perused his body, I began to realize Cole had a lot more going on under that work uniform I'm used to seeing him in. As if reading my mind, his crystal blue eyes crinkle at the sides, as his beautiful thick pink lips lift into a sexy smile. I watch as he raises his beer to me. I have to make myself look away, "Lord, have mercy." I murmur under my breath as I turn to go look for Shell, I need a drink. As if she was summoned, I turned around to find my bestie with a tequila shot in each hand. She offers me one before drinking the other herself. That was the first of many that night. I definitely achieved my goal. I enjoyed my forty-fifth birthday to the fullest.

CHAPTER NINE

August 18, 2013

Sam

I slowly open my eyes, blinking a few times, trying to orient myself. Looking up at the familiar ceiling, I realize I'm in my bedroom. What the hell happened last night? I try sitting up, but with my arms feeling like jelly, all I do is flop back down. I instantly realize two things: I have a hangover with very little recollection of what happened last night, which is pretty odd for me, and I'm naked. Not remembering much aside from having a good time, I vaguely remember Lance and Gio saying bye to me before leaving to catch their flight. Lance made sure he was back in my good graces before he left. I smile, remembering his gift, a bottle of Clase Azul Reposado. It's an ultra-premium reposado tequila I've been dying to add to my collection for a while now. He and Gio both went out of their way to make sure I was enjoying myself. I don't remember much after that. Gingerly, I shake my head, trying to clear it. Deciding to rest a bit more before getting up, I lay back down. My mind wanders back to my naked body. "Who in the hell took off my clothes?" I wonder out loud. We were still partying when Lance left, so it couldn't have been him. Now anxious to find out, I say, "Alexa, call LJ."

"Calling LJ."

"Hey, Ma, how are you feeling this fine morning?" he says after a laugh.

"Boy, shut up, and tell me what happened last night." I croak out, sounding like I swallowed a frog.

"Well, since you asked so nicely, you and your friends were a delight to watch drunk. I had to put one of your shirts on Shell. She kept falling out of her bathing suit. I started to think it was intentional after the 5th time I had to readjust her suit."

I try to laugh but instantly regret the slight movement as the pounding in my head intensified. "How did the party end?" I croak out, massaging my temples.

"Shell took off your clothes and got you all tucked in. After everyone was gone, Jay helped me straighten up a bit and take the trash out. I made sure you were ok before setting the alarm and heading out. I dropped Aunt Shell off at home because Cassie had to leave the party early to drive up north for work. Oh, and I got Killa with me. I didn't want him disturbing you while you were trying to sleep. Call me when you're ready for him, and I'll bring him back with some hot coffee. "

"Thank you, baby, for taking such good care of me," I mumble my appreciation.

"Do you think I would do anything less? You're my mama. I got you."

I laugh despite the pain, "Thank you again, baby. I'm going back to sleep."

"Alright, Ma, call me when you're up. And ma?"

"Yes?"

"Happy birthday again."

"Thank you, Sonshine. Enjoy your day, ok?" I promptly pulled the covers over my head and drifted back to sleep.

A few hours later, I showered and felt good as new... Well, maybe that's pushing it. I haven't told LJ to bring Killa home just yet. I wanted to thoroughly clean my house first, which wasn't easy because of how hungover I was. I almost gave up a few times. After making myself a light dinner, I sat on the sofa and watched tv. Just when I'm getting into *You* on Netflix, the phone rings. Sighing, I grab the phone off the table to see Eboni flash across the screen. "What could she possibly want?" I murmur, tempted not to pick up.

"Hey, love?" I answer and wait to hear her reason for calling.

"Hey, birthday girl, how are you feeling today?"

"Pretty good now. I wasn't feeling so hot this morning. I was still nursing the after-effects from last night."

'Well, that's good to hear because we want to come by to pick you up and take you shopping!" Eboni finishes with a squeal, barely able to contain her excitement.

"We as in?" I leave off, not having the slightest idea who she's talking about.

"Me, mom, and Emoni girl. Who else would I be talking about?" she ends with a laugh.

As soon as she mentioned my mother, I knew I would decline this disaster waiting to happen. I can see it now, it's my birthday, but somehow we'll end up in all the stores with clothes that fit them. I will end up sitting in a chair by the dressing room as my sisters and probably my mother go in and out of the dressing room wanting my opinion. I will eventually get hungry and let them know I will meet up with them at the food court. And right before I left the store, I would hear my mother say after me. *"Make sure you only get a salad, Sam. Lord knows you don't need to eat anything else from there."*

Yeah. I have no desire to subject myself to that, so I kindly say, "That is so sweet of you for thinking of me, but I'm going to stay around the house today and clean. Also, LJ will be bringing Killa home shortly, and you already know I have to bathe him as soon as he gets here. I don't know all the places LJ had my baby today."

"I swear, Sam, I am so sick of you and that damn dog. You're really going to turn down a day of shopping for a dog?" I can practically hear her eyes rolling.

"Stop it. You already know Killa is my baby. He is just as much your nephew as LJ. I've told you before to stop treating him like an outsider. It hurts his feelings." I finish with a chuckle.

"That damn rat is no kin to me, but fine, I will tell mom and Emoni you won't be able to join us. Mom is going to be so disappointed." She finishes in that whiny voice of hers, making me cringe.

"I'm sure she will recover quickly," I say dryly while rolling my eyes. "You guys have fun, and give mom and Emoni my love."

"Ok, girl, I will call you later." She says before hanging up. Letting out a relieved sigh, I grab the remote and press play to finish watching my show.

CHAPTER TEN

November 5, 2013
3 months later

"Pregnant! What do you mean, I'm pregnant, Joann?" Feeling hot, I close my eyes and count to ten. Trying to slow my palpitating heart and rising panic, I open my eyes and try again, "There is absolutely no way I can be pregnant. Lance and I have followed the rhythm method with one-hundred-percent success for all these years. You already know that because you counseled us on this method all those years ago, remember?" I ask, hopeful. "Lance damn near has his Ph.D. in the method. There has got to be some mistake. Please, Joann, run the test again because this is not possible." As I finish, I'm breathing hard, looking into my O.B.'s sympathetic eyes as she nods patiently and listens to me fall apart.

Two hours later, I'm sitting in my car, just numb. After triple-checking the results, I've had to realize that there's no mistake. I am pregnant, twelve weeks to be exact. *How is this even possible? Did Lance and I make love before he and Gio left for that business trip?* From the date of conception, Joann is telling me, that's around the time it would have been, sometime around my birthday. Shaking my head, I realize that couldn't be possible; that was during a red light time in my cycle. I would have been fertile, and Lance wouldn't have touched me with a ten-foot pole if he thought there was any chance I could get pregnant.

I drop my head in my hands, feeling like I'm in an alternate universe. All these questions begin to assault me at once. *What am I going to do? How am I going to tell Lance? Will he believe I honestly don't know how this even happened?* One thought pushes all others out of my head, leaving me paralyzed with fear, *"What if he leaves me?"* "Oh God," I say on a choked sop. So riddled with fear and confusion, all I can do is lay my head against the steering wheel and cry my heart out.

After my mini-meltdown, I try to examine this with a clear mind. I think back over the past few weeks and what led me to go in to see Joanne in the first place. I noticed I was doing quite a bit of belching. Shell brought it to my attention when we met up a couple of weeks back to catch a movie. I damn near belched through the whole movie. Shell finally leaned over and asked, "girl, are you alright?" It was so embarrassing. I made sure we were out of there before anyone else started leaving out the movie.

I also took note of an abnormally light period I had last month. I decided it was time to make an appointment to see Joann. Never in a million years would I have thought she would come back and say I was pregnant! I think absently, shaking my head. Driving home, I think over my options. Maybe I should have Joanne schedule me for an abortion. That way, I won't have to explain anything to anyone. How can I explain something I don't even understand myself? After driving in silence for a while, I begin to laugh, realizing this is nonsense. I know my husband, whatever happens, whatever this is, Lance and I will get through it together. Feeling a bit more in control, I send him a text message telling him we need to talk and to meet me at home.

My heart starts to pound once I turn down our street and see his truck parked in the driveway. Walking into the kitchen, I absently place my purse on the counter and listen out for him. I sluggishly made my way up to our bedroom. Starting to feel lightheaded, I look down and realize my hands are shaking. Taking in a couple of deep breaths, I reach out and grab the banister for support.

"Hey, baby, what's up? Lance says as I walk into our bedroom. I close my eyes and pray for strength. I take a deep breath and proceed to tell him that I'm twelve weeks pregnant.

CHAPTER ELEVEN

Sam

"Come on, Samantha! you're trying to tell me you're pregnant, and it ain't my baby, do I look like a fool to you?" Lance says forcefully, as my watery eyes track him as he paces back and forth. "Please help me try to understand this shit. It's kind of hard to believe that you haven't stepped out on me, on our marriage!" he yells, hitting his chest with force. "Please lead me in the direction of the truth, right now!" Make this shit make sense, Sam!

He lets out a heavy sigh, before falling back into the chair next to our bed. Taking in the utter confusion on my husband's face, I go to him, lowering myself between his legs and trying again to explain this bizarre situation. "Lance, I…" putting my head down while breathing deeply, I try to calm my racing heart before continuing. "Like I've said to you before, yes, I'm twelve weeks pregnant, but baby, I have no idea how that came to be. Listen to me," I say, trying to take his large hand in mine, but he snatches it away as if it's poisonous. Hurt deeply by his rejection, I continue. "We've been married for over twenty beautiful years, twenty years, Lance! We..." I pause to clear my dry throat before trying again. "We have a wonderful life together. A wonderful son, hell, even our dog is obscenely happy. We've built this amazing life together. I wouldn't jeopardize the love we have for nothing or no one. Baby, I need you. Please, Lance," I beg as my voice breaks, "I need you to believe me. I need my husband, my protector, my best friend because, baby, I'm so scared." I finish in a trembling voice as tears roll unchecked down my face.

As he remains silent, I swallow hard, trying to pull myself together before continuing. "When Joann told me I was pregnant, my first thought was there had to be some mistake. There's no way that was even possible. "I pause once more while looking down at the carpet as if the answer I'm looking for may be found there. Bringing my head back up to him, I continue, "The... estimated date of conception, Joann told me, was around our "unsafe days," but you already know this, we usually abstain from sex or use a condom. This has worked for us for years. Lance."

I close my eyes as we sit quietly for a while. I pull air deep into my lungs before allowing it to slowly leave my lips. "I'm forty-five, and you're forty-nine," I softly say, looking down at my quaking hands. "I know it's well past the time for me to have another baby. The only baby I'm waiting for is our beautiful grandbaby our son will give us one day."

I laugh softly to try to lighten the mood. I know my husband is trying to process all of this. Hell, I'm trying my hardest to process it as well. After another long stretch of silence, he lets out a long ragged sigh. He pats me on my shoulder so that I can make room for him to stand. My heart sinks when he walks into our closet and comes out carrying two of his suitcases. Once he lays them on the bed, he turns to me with his hands on his hips, his lips held tightly together. Once he starts to speak, my heart breaks so loud that I have the urge to put my hand to my ear to see if there's actual blood. It's a good thing I'm still kneeling because my knees would have surely given out with the realization that my best friend didn't believe me… and was leaving me.

CHAPTER TWELVE

Sam

"I've always accepted you the way you are, flaws and all. I know what I look like, and know we don't match, but I still tried to love you and build a life with you, and this is how you repay me?!

"Well, whoever you are pregnant by," he says, chuckling, "I hope he makes you happy because when he realizes just how weak your fat ass is, I promise you, he will be gone. And then what are you going to do? Who's going to want you? A forty-five-year-old, fat single mother. Yeah, good luck with that," were Lance's parting words.

I'm broken. Every breath I take, I pray it was my last. Lance leaving me wasn't the thing that destroyed me. It was the fact he did not believe me. I tried my best to make him see the truth. I will never forget the way he looked at me when he stepped over my broken body. "That man is my life. Doesn't he realize I will give my life for his?" I gasp out. I can't see how I will be able to go on without him. I know that makes me weak and pathetic, but I don't give a damn at this point. I'm lost without him.

I don't know how long I've stayed like that on the floor. Absently, I turn my heavy head towards the window. I can see the sun had set, and the clear California night sky now twinkled brightly with stars. Willing my body to move took great effort as I slowly peel myself off the floor. I feel my stomach rumble, reminding me I haven't eaten anything in hours. As soon as the thought turns to my stomach, I immediately think about the small parasite that has invaded my body and destroyed my life in seconds. Something that literally came out of nowhere, and caused this amount of damage, has got to be pure evil. *"I GOT TO GET IT OUT!* my mind screams in my head, prompting me to move. I run into my bathroom with a single thought, get this thing out of me now! I pause when I catch a glimpse of myself in the mirror. My breath catches when I hear it *"Mmm... You just taste so damn good, baby,"* I hear Lance's voice in my fractured mind, causing my image to distort as tears fill my eyes. *"Green-light, baby?"* His whispers continue taunting me, *"I'm nothing without you, Samantha."* He finishes as his voice fades.

Suddenly, the sound of a wounded animal split my ears. It didn't register that it was me making that god-awful sound as I continued to scream uncontrollably. "I'm not what you need, Lance!" I yell as I begin to attack myself. "You can do so much better than an old fat insecure woman with mommy issues!" I scream as I claw at any part of my body I can sink my nails into. I think of the thing growing inside of me, and instantly, I'm clawing at my stomach to get it out. In a blind rage, my mind isn't capable of registering the deep wounds I'm inflicting on myself. A dark thought cloaks my battered mind, stunning me, *"Lance has a straight razor in his Louis Vuitton toiletry bag I got him for Father's Day.* "Running like a crazy woman into my husband's bathroom, I locate the bag on the sink. Rushing to it, I ripped the zipper down and plunged my hands inside, searching for my tool of redemption. Because of my blind rage, I never felt the razor as it began slicing into my fingers as I aggressively rummaged through the bag.

Only after noticing everything becoming slippery and bright

red did I finally realize I was cut. Numb to the pain, one clear thought continuously bombards my mind: *GET IT OUT*. I frantically fumble to open the razor with quaking hands. Once achieved, I try my best to secure a good grip, but it's damn near impossible with my bloodied, slippery hands. As I'm about to make the first slice into my body, strong hands grab both my wrists from behind. As I look up into the mirror, my crazed eyes barely make out the image through my tears. A beautiful brown face comes into focus. "Lance, baby, you came back. Please tell me you believe me." I cry harder as relief washes over me so swiftly I'm dizzy. As I blink away my tears, the face becomes clearer to me. It's not my husband I thought coming to rescue me.

I blink a couple more times and gasp as my son's anguished face comes into focus. Something shifts deep inside me, watching tears stream down his face. My frenzied mind cleared enough for me to hear his words. "Mama" he screams! "What the hell are you doing to yourself? We have to get you to the hospital. You're hurt, Ma. Please drop the blade." Finally registering my numb hands as LJ continues to hold my wrist tightly, I drop the razor. He immediately turns me around and pulls me into his body. My son is not a small man; feeling my baby shaking as if he were a little boy clears the rest of my mind of the manic fog. As he's crying deep, racking sobs, he tells me how much he needs me, that I'm his best friend, and he couldn't live without me. After a few minutes of us standing like that, I pat him on the back to let him know I'm better and ready to talk, but as soon as I'm released from his strong arms, everything goes black.

CHAPTER THIRTEEN

LJ

I catch my mother just before she hits the floor. Scooping her up into my arms, I hurry out of the bathroom to get her some medical attention.

I was out on the job with Cole when I received a call from my father. "Hey Cole, I need to take this," I shout, holding up my phone.

"No worries, boss man, this small ass dentist office I could have handled myself, you know that, right?" He asks, eyeing me. It was true. Only one of my guys was needed for this small job. I figured it would be that much quicker with two.

"Thanks, man," I tell him, heading towards the back of the office. "What's up, pop?" I say after hitting talk. Met with silence, I look at the screen to make sure the call hadn't dropped. "Pop, you there?"

"Hey, son," is my father's low reply, instantly putting me on alert. I wait for him to continue, not wanting to push. I'm extremely anxious nonetheless. Finally, he begins to speak, and what he says floors me.

"Your mom and I have decided to call it quits, LJ."

Not sure I heard him correctly, I remain quiet, not wanting to miss a single word he has to say. In my shock, I vaguely hear, *"I'm going to be staying at the Marriott, off San Carlos in Belmont."*

"Come by and see me tonight so we can talk. I love you, son. I'm sorry we failed you." With that, he ended the call. As my mind comes back online, I try to comprehend the things he did NOT say. A voice screams in my head for me to get to my mother. NOW!

"Cole! Cole! Man, we gotta go!" I yell, hurrying towards the front. "Somethings up with my mother. We gotta go now!" I didn't even realize my hands were shaking until Cole took the keys out of my hand. He patted me on the back and told me, *"he's got this,"* while pushing me towards the door. After he finishes locking up the building, he runs and hops into the driver's seat as I get in on the passenger side. We are in one of the company trucks, but Cole still manages to get us to moms in record time. I hop out of the truck before it even stops, instantly hearing her screams from inside the house. Thank God the front door is unlocked, preventing me from breaking it down. I take three steps at a time, determined to get to her.

I don't have to search for her upstairs, her pitiful wails lead me to my father's bathroom. When I get to the door, what I see stops my heart. My beautiful mother looks ravaged. She has deep angry scratches all over her face, chest, and arms. When her shirt parts in the front, I am able to get a better look at her chest and stomach from her reflection in the mirror. It looks like she had been mauled by a wild animal. Hot with anger, I spun around to go search for the attacker, ready to tear them apart with my bare hands. But, before I can, I catch a glimpse of something silver in her hand. Fear like I've never felt before launches me forward. I grab her wrists right as she is about to slide the razor into herself.

I don't know how long we stand like that. I don't even

realize I'm squeezing her wrists as tightly as I am until they go limp from lack of blood circulation. As the realization hit me, it steals my next breath. My mother, my heart, is trying to take her own life.

I don't realize Cole is right behind me until I turn and see him standing there with the comforter from my parents' bed in his hands. I carefully transfer her into his arms, before turning to lead the way. We race downstairs, and through the kitchen. I snatch her key fob, off the counter and rush to open the garage. Cole, never missing a beat, rushes past me and carefully places her in the back seat of her car. I slide in the back with her, carefully placing her head on my lap, trying to make her as comfortable as possible. Briefly taking my eyes off of her, I look up to see Cole sprinting back into the garage after closing the doors in the house. As Cole slides behind the wheel, I notice for the first time how hard he is breathing. Everybody loves my Mama. I know this is tearing him up seeing her like this. *"Please, God,"* I silently prayed, leaning my head back against the headrest trying to swallow the golf ball in my throat. *"Please let my mama be ok."*

CHAPTER FOURTEEN

Act 2

Sam

Joann is an amazing and extremely busy doctor. Yet she decides to come to my hospital room daily to personally change my dressings. I have several more than capable nurses that come in throughout the day that could handle this minor task, but Joann always insists on doing it herself. She always comes in with the supplies she needs to complete the task in silence, then she leaves. I've come to realize it's her way to reassure herself that I'm ok. So, I sit there in silence, taking comfort in her gentle hand and peaceful presence as she checks on my rapidly-healing injuries. The day after I arrived at the hospital, I woke to an elderly woman sitting in a chair tucked in the corner. Her head was down as if she was reading something.

"Hello," I say with a gravelly voice.

As she looks up, I'm greeted with kind blue eyes and a gentle smile.

"Good, you're awake!! How are you feeling, Samantha? Let's

get you some water. I bet you're probably parched." She says, making her way to her feet.

Not wanting to bother the kind woman, I raise my hand to stop her efforts." That's very kind of you," I croak out, "but I'm sure I can call the nurse."

"Oh, that's nonsense." She swats my suggestion away with the flick of her hand. "I'm right here and more than capable of retrieving you some water, my dear."

Instantly feeling my ears warm, I smile and say, "Thank you."

She raises my bed into a comfortable sitting position before rolling the hospital table close.

"Now, this is a fresh pitcher of water the nurse just brought in." The sweet little lady informs while pouring some into a cup and adding a straw.

"Take it easy, ok, don't go too fast," she says, bringing the straw to my lips.

After taking a few sips, my throat is lubricated enough to clear it. Testing my voice, I tell her, "thank you, I needed that." Smiling at this angel of a woman.

"You're probably wondering who I am?" she asks, chuckling while walking back to her chair to pull it next to my bed.

I want to stop her and call for assistance, but I have a feeling that wouldn't have gone over too well. So, I wait patiently for her to finish her task and listen to what she's about to say.

Once settled, she begins, "Samantha, I'm Dr. Rosenthal. I'm a Psychologist here at San Ramon Medical Center. Dr. Joann King asked if I could speak with you. She's extremely concerned about you and your unborn child." She finishes with concern shimmering in her crystal blue eyes.

At the mention of the baby, my mind relives what I almost did. "Oh my god, my baby!" Not the little mystery that currently resides in my uterus, my grown baby, LJ How traumatized he must have been, finding me like that. With my eyes tightly shut,

I cover my mouth, trying to keep my scream at bay. Tears begin to fall unchecked down my face.

"Now, now, Samantha," Dr. Rosenthal says while rubbing my arm. "No need to relive all that, but I would like to know how you feel if that's ok? You can share as much or as little as you like. Does that work?"

Taking deep breaths, I begin to relax, hearing her gentle words. Nodding my head, I begin to speak.

Over the next week, I was visited daily by Dr. Rosenthal, as well as Joann's continued personal care. On the day I was to be released, Joann came in, in full Dr mode. Her previously stressed and worried eyes now reflect her shrewd intellect.

"I received Dr. Rosenthal's report earlier today." She tells me while flipping through my chart to locate the report.

"She has cleared you to be released. She believes you are of sound mind and do not pose a threat to yourself or your unborn child. She also recommends you continue with outpatient therapy with either herself or someone of your choosing. As for the pregnancy, we perform abortions up until twenty-three weeks in my clinic, so you still have time if that's what you choose. There's also an amazing adoption agency I can refer you to. And lastly, if you decide to keep the baby, being that you're forty-five, there are some risks associated with having a baby later in life. There are also additional tests that are offered to older pregnant women. Of course, you could also opt-out altogether. I will make sure you are fully informed to make the best decision for you."

Finally, putting the clipboard down, she looks into my eyes, "and if you decide to keep the baby, I will personally do my very best to ensure mom is healthy and we deliver a healthy baby. And if at any time it all becomes too much, or you feel like you want to harm yourself again, please please call me." She says with raw emotion.

She takes a minute to get her emotions under control before

continuing. Clearing her throat, she says, "I've written you a prescription for prenatal vitamins and iron pills. Your labs show you're a bit anemic. Shell's downstairs picking them up now. I've also scheduled you for a prenatal appointment in my clinic two weeks from now. We can talk about what you decide to do about the pregnancy then." She finishes with a knowing smile, "you are strong, Sam. You will get through this."

"I also have to inform you. I ordered a rape kit when you arrived, and that came back inconclusive. I didn't detect any DNA other than Lance's. I figured that would have been the case, being that this occurred a few months ago, but it was worth a shot. Your home surveillance shows no signs of forced entry or being tampered with. I know this is all bizarre, but I believe you, and I'm here, ok?"

As I'm trying to process all this information, I can only think about one thing… "Do you think I can do this alone, Joann?" I whisper so quietly that I'm amazed she even heard me.

"Yes! Without a doubt, it will get easier, Sam, I promise.

After Joann leaves, I rest my head against the pillow. Looked at the birds right outside my window. Finally coming to grips with the hard truth, Lance is gone, and I'm pregnant and have no clue who the father is.

There is one thing that I know for sure. Nothing will ever be the same again.

CHAPTER FIFTEEN

Sam

"Listen, Sam, his ass was no damn good in the first place."

"Shell, please," I weakly say, not ready to talk about Lance.

Looking over at me in the passenger seat, she continues as if she didn't hear me. "No, girl, you need to hear this, especially now."

"I mean, yes, it was extremely shocking to hear that you were pregnant."

I rolled my eyes, leaned my head back against the headrest, and listened to her unwanted rant.

"But when you swore to me on all things holy, you didn't have an affair, I believed you." Looking at me, she gives me a silly look with a wink.

More seriously, she continues, "That's just not in your character, Sam, and anyone that knows you can attest to that. Even Lance, sorry ass." She finishes.

"Alright!" She abruptly changes the subject while she launches us into traffic, "Let's get you home, mama."

I rolled my head her way and just stared.

I didn't have to say a word as she answered my unspoken question, *"Really, Shell?"*

"I'm sorry, I'm sorry." She says, holding up her hands in mock surrender.

"You know I've always called you mama, so don't look at me like that." She chuckles. "Plus, you're going to have to lighten up, girl, or this is going to be a long-ass nine months for every-body." She says the last part under her breath.

"Have you talked to LJ?" I ask, trying to change the subject.

"Yep, he's meeting us at my house, with some of your things and your hamster."

"Don't look at me like that, Sam. You know I'm only speaking the truth." She says as I cut my eyes at her for talking about my baby like that.

"You already know how I feel about that little ass dog. I don't know why you didn't just get a hamster if you were going to get something that damn small. Makes no damn sense. I know if I was a big dog, I would be offended." She grumbles to herself, causing me to laugh.

I lay my head back and tune my crazy friend out. I close my eyes and try not to think about Lance or being pregnant.

CHAPTER SIXTEEN

November 14th

Sam

I stir when I feel a light kiss being placed on my cheek. "Come on, mama, let's get you inside so you can rest."

My eyes popped open the moment I heard my son's voice. I notice he's crouched down with the car door already opened. While looking into his warm brown eyes, I had to remember the promise I made to myself in the hospital. I promised I would keep it together when I finally laid eyes on him. Taking in a shaky breath, I'm finally able to say what's been on my mind for days.

"Baby, I'm sorry…"

"Mama, you don't…"

I held my hand up to stop him so that I could finish.

"Yes, I do, sweetie. I owe you an apology. I'm so ashamed, LJ. I had a moment of weakness that I truly regret now. But I promise you. It will never happen again. I will never leave you. I need you to know that your mama is not weak." taking a breath,

I continue, "I have some decisions to make, and I want you a part of them, every step of the way. I won't keep any secrets, ok?"

With trembling lips, my son nods his head and helps me out of the car. Once I'm out, he pulls me straight into his arms. We stay like that for a while, me rubbing his back as his tears soak my shirt at my shoulder. Not caring one bit, I need my son to know that his mother is strong. Feeling a tug at the hem of my dress, excitement zips through me before looking down.

"Killa!" I scream, bending down to scoop him up. "Hi, baby, mama missed you," I say, as happy tears slide down my face.

"Really, Samantha, really?!" I hear Shell say from behind, causing me to roll my eyes. "You're really going to break down over a damn dog. I would be pissed if I was you, LJ. Just disrespectful." Looking as though she's just too through, she turns and walks off.

LJ and I can't help but laugh as we follow her inside her lavish home.

CHAPTER SEVENTEEN

Sam

"What do you want to do, Ma? LJ asks as we lounge in one of Shell's plush guest rooms.

"I spent days at the house when this first happened. I checked everything. I had the cops come out to see if they could uncover something I was overlooking.

"I know, Joann told me."

"You don't remember anything out of the ordinary around that time?"

"Nope." I express, releasing a frustrated sigh.

"Ma, I hate to ask you this," he says, running his hands down his face. "But are you one hundred percent sure it's not dad's baby?

I know he was hoping it was his father's baby, not because he wants us to stay together but because he just wants Lance to stop all the negative talk he's been spewing about me.

"Yes, baby, I'm sure. I also don't remember anything out of the ordinary. I've gone over every detail hundreds of times around my birthday weekend, and nothing strikes me as odd."

"Mama…"

"Yeah, son?" I say, giving him my undivided attention.

"We got this, ok? You already know I got your back no matter what. So do Aunt Shell and Uncle Gio. Even the guys at work. Oh, yeah, Mason told me to tell you, he's all in, whatever that means."

We both laugh, thinking about Mason before LJ continues.

"Just forget about everything else, especially my sorry-ass father."

"LJ!" I gasp!

"I'm sorry, Ma, I just can't with that dude right now. Thinking about how he just left you makes my blood boil."

"LJ, he was shocked and upset, I…"

"Don't do that, Ma," he says, shaking his head. "Don't take up for him. Anyone that knows you would have known you were speaking the truth, no matter how bizarre the circumstance."

Pausing, he looks down before continuing.

Not meeting my eyes, he says, "I saw how he lit into you after you explained the situation."

My head snapped up in my son's direction.

As if reading my mind, he replies, "Yes, I saw what happened, Ma. When I was going through the home surveillance footage trying to find something, I saw and heard what happened that day from the hall camera."

Too ashamed to continue holding his gaze, I look down at my hands in my lap.

I clear my throat, and I say, "I'm sorry you had to see that, son."

"Mama, look at me."

I try to summon the courage to do as he asks.

"It's me, remember? You don't have to be ashamed or embarrassed about any of this, you hear me?"

Somewhat relieved by his words, I nod.

With a gruff voice, he continues.

"You will always have me, mama. I never want you to feel as hopeless as you felt that day. Seeing you so broken broke my heart. You just wanted him to believe you, Ma. I could actually feel what you were saying through the video. How could he just leave you like that? I saw your eyes. You were telling him the truth. You ALWAYS tell the truth. He knows that! I will never forgive him!" His voice vibrated with anger.

"LJ, baby, please calm down." I express to him with mounting concern.

"No, mama, that was low down, and he did that to my mother! He slaps his chest to express his pain.

"LJ, please!" I desperately say, unable to take a second more of my son's anguish.

He lets out a long breath before saying, "I'm ok, Ma. I'm going to head out." He says, pointing towards the door, "I have to stop by the shop. We've been one man down for the past week.

"Which one of the guys is it? Is everything ok?" I ask, with concern covering my face, as I momentarily push my dilemma to the side.

"Yeah, it's Cole. He had a family emergency. He'll be back on Friday.

"Oh, ok, that's good," I say

"I will call you later, ok." He leans down to place a kiss on my cheek before walking out the room. I know my son is hurting. I pray that, with time, we both can heal.

CHAPTER EIGHTEEN

November 16th

Sam

"Samantha!" I hear my name being yelled,

"What in the hell could she possibly want this early in the morning," I say under my breath. I glance at the clock to make sure it is, in fact, as early as it feels.

"Yep, just as I thought, 7:04 AM." I groan as I roll into a sitting position.

I hear Shell's big ass mouth once again.

"Samantha!"

I took in a deep breath and yelled, "I'm coming. so stop calling me heffa!" Hearing her laughter at my grumping response makes me smile.

"Well, bitch, hurry up." I hear her say it a bit lower. Laughing, I bend my body into a delicious stretch before heading into the bathroom to freshen up. I've been here recuperating for the past two weeks. It's been nice spending time with my bestie, but I think it's time for me to head home. I have to start dealing with life. Coming out of the bathroom, I set Killa on the floor before grabbing my cell phone and heading in the direction of the delicious smell of bacon. Glancing at my phone, I see I have two new text messages from Gio. Seeing his name instantly brings a smile to my face. He has checked on me every single day since I've been here. He was a little disappointed, I wouldn't let him come over to see for himself that I was really ok. I just really didn't want him to see me until some of the worst scratches had healed.

"What do your loud ass want?" I say to her, walking into the kitchen. "And the only reason I'm here is that I couldn't resist the smell of bacon."

"I'm making us some breakfast. I also wanted to talk to you about something, so come have a seat." She pointed towards the table with her spatula in her hand.

"Uh, oh, this sounds serious. Am I in trouble?" I jokingly ask.

"Girl shut up." She laughs.

I sit down and wait for my friend to begin.

With her back to me, she's quiet for a minute before she starts to speak. "You know I don't talk much about my past, because it's just that—*the past*. I don't believe in wasting precious time or energy on something that can't be changed. With that being said, I want to talk to you about my mother."

This takes me completely by surprise because Shell never talks about that woman. I know she wasn't in Shell or Cassie's life. I just never knew why.

"My mother was something else, Sam. One of the most selfish people I've ever met in my life. She always put her needs and the needs of her men before her daughters. Marie Johnson had to have herself a man, Chile. She laughs without humor. "She would literally have a nervous breakdown every time a man left her. The ambulance would have to be called, and she would end up in a mental hospital every time. This was her cycle. Not caring every time she did this, she was leaving her two young daughters to fend for themselves.

She goes quiet to collect her thoughts as she prepares our plates with bacon, eggs, homemade potatoes, and orange juice. I notice she places a prenatal and iron pill on a napkin for me. Normally, I would have made a snide remark, but I thought it best to keep quiet.

Once seated in her seat, she continues.

"I had enough when one of her boyfriend's made his way into my bedroom one night. I stabbed his ass in the thigh before he could take what he wanted. As traumatic as that night was, the most devastating part was that my mother believed him when he told her I tried to seduce him, girl!" What could my young fourteen-year-old ass possibly know about seducing a grown man?" She asks, not expecting an answer.

I sit across from my dearest friend with my mouth wide open. I want to go to her to comfort her, but I think I am too shocked and filled with dread to move.

Oblivious to my catatonic state, she continues. "I was fourteen at the time, and Cassie was four. I took her, and we moved in with my grandmother. It was extremely crowded because many family members lived in that tiny apartment. I made a promise to myself that night. That I would get me and Cassie out of there, I would make sure we were always safe, and above everything else, never depend on a man for happiness. As a young girl, watching and realizing that my mother's happiness was directly tied to some man, I vowed never to give another person that much power over me over my happiness."

"Oh, Shell..." I finally respond, with sorrow heavy in my voice. She holds up her hand to stop me from saying more.

"Listen, I'm telling you this because hearing and seeing what happened to you took me back to the fourteen-year-old scared girl from Watts. That just wanted her mother, that hasn't crossed my mind in years." She finishes with a haunted expression in her eyes.

She closes her eyes as tears run down her beautiful mahogany face. She continues, "You can never lose yourself like that ever again. Not over a man, or anyone for that matter. You're too amazing and have way too much to live for. Do you hear me?" "You're having a baby... so what. You've wanted another one for years, but Lance's selfish ass took it upon himself and made the decision for both of you. You got another chance to be a mother, Sam. Try to find happiness in that," she finishes.

I'm out of my chair and pulled her into my arms before she even opened her eyes.

I'm going to try, but it's difficult to be happy when you don't know how you even got pregnant. All I feel is fear.

CHAPTER NINETEEN

November 17th

Sam

"Make sure you call me, no scratch that, make sure you FaceTime me often. Let me know how you're doing. Also, let me know when your next prenatal appointment is ok?"

"Yes, Shell, I understand all of your instructions," I state, hugging my friend goodbye.

"Are you sure you don't want to stay awhile longer? You don't think you may be rushing things?" She says, with concern in her voice.

I leaned back and looked into my dearest friend's eyes. "No, Shell, you've restored me to health. It's time for me to go home and face what's ahead of me, but thank you, girl. You, and Cassie, have been amazing. Please give her a big hug and a kiss for me when you see her, ok?"

I hurried to get inside the car before Shell could start her pleas for me to stay all over again. I've enjoyed being here, but I'm ready to be home.

Before going home, LJ and I stopped by the hospital to pick up a copy of my medical records. I will be going through everything with a fine-tooth comb. Yesterday was my first prenatal appointment. I met with, or rather Shell, LJ, Gio, and I met with Joann to go over my labs. Once I informed her of my decision to keep the baby, we talked about the different tests available for women my age. The risks and advantages of each, as well if I wanted to opt-out of them altogether. I left there feeling more informed and also knowing that the baby and I are doing fine.

As I walked through my front door, it was kind of a surreal moment. I waited for the crushing despair to hit me, but it never came. I did feel a bit of sadness, but the sheer happiness of being home countered that.

"Be careful, Killa!" I say, laughing as he rips around the house. He's definitely just as happy to be home as I am.

"Come on, Ma, let's get you into bed so that you can get some rest," LJ says, bringing the rest of my luggage inside.

"I'm feeling pretty good, babe. I was thinking about cleaning up a bit before finding something to cook this evening."

"You don't have to worry about anything, Ma. I ordered dinner from that Italian restaurant you love, and the cleaners came in a couple of days ago. I made sure I was here the whole time they were here cleaning."

As I look into my son's troubled eyes, I know he needs reassurance.

"Baby, everything is going to be ok. I'm going to be ok. Do you understand? I have faith we're going to get to the bottom of this, but what we are not going to do is become so distrustful of everyone it affects our lives, ok?"

"Yes, ma'am, but could you please do me this one favor and just take it easy today? We can do whatever you want tomorrow, ok?" He finishes with pleading eyes.

Laughing, I can only agree with that heartfelt plea.

"Sure, son."

CHAPTER TWENTY

November 24th,

"Teresa... TERESA!" I yell while gathering my things.

"Yes, Ms. Johnson?" my assistant answers, poking her head into my office.

"I'm sorry for yelling," I say, rubbing the bridge of my nose. "I just wanted to let you know I'm about to head home. There's not much I can do on our end until we hear back from the listing agent for the Saint Claire property. If Mr. Grant calls giving you a hard time, you can forward him to me." I finish with a heavy sigh.

"No worries, Ms. Johnson, I can handle Mr. Grant if he calls. You go home and get some rest, ok?" She says with sad eyes. Everyone in the office knows Sam and how close we are. They don't know the specifics of what happened to her, but they knew she had been recuperating at my house. Today is my first day back in the office. I've been working from my home office to make sure I was at my besties' beck and call.

"Thank you, Tee. If he gets too out of line, remind him of the options I gave him the last time he tried to pull that rich billionaire entitlement bullshit." I laugh out loud. "I'm the only person that can get that property he so desperately desires, and he knows this. Sometimes I have to remind him of that."

Grabbing my things off my desk, I head out the door. I stop in the doorway to pop a kiss on Teresa's cheek. "Thank you, girl. I'm going home to take a hot bath and drink a whole bottle of wine."

I rushed out the door, walking on autopilot towards my parking spot. My steps falter when I see a white card sticking out from my windshield wiper. Quickly glancing around the parking lot, I walked over to pluck it off. Turning it over, I see three beautifully written words.

"Miss Me Yet?"

"What the hell?" I murmur, confused, as I turn the card over to see if there's anything else on it. Catching a familiar scent that wafted off the card, I brought it to my nose and inhaled. I instantly smell the delicious, unforgettable scent of Rodney Adams. With a smile tugging at my lips, I look around one last time before unlocking my car and climbing inside. Putting all my things on the passenger side, I take a cleansing breath and lean back against the seat. Looking down at the card in my hand, I think about the last time I saw him.

While circling her supple hips to maximize the pleasure she was currently feeling, Shell lets her head fall back, allowing her waist-length dreadlocks to cascade down her back. A soft sensual moan leaves her lips, taking with it the rest of her frustration from the hectic day she's had. Rodney knew just what she needed. He and his big beautiful dick were waiting for her when she walked through the door. "Do you like that, baby?" I say with a sigh, looking down into his gorgeous gray eyes. I seductively rock my wet pussy over his talented mouth as I ride his face. His answer came with a deep moan as he clamps his thick lips around my clit, and sucks hard. I feel myself begin to unravel when his large hands clamp down onto my thighs, preventing my escape as he devours me.

Stepping out of the shower, I can't stop the smile that plays on my lips. Rodney's lovemaking will keep a girl smiling for weeks. "He's such a dirty boy," I say out loud to no one. One of the reasons I just can't get enough. Feeling refreshed and super relaxed, I don't bother grabbing my kimono robe from behind the door as I walk into my closet to finish getting ready for the night.

"So this is what you do when nobody's here? Walk around naked, showcasing that luscious body." I hear a deep voice say from behind me.

"You still here?" I absently glanced over my shoulder before reaching for my favorite moisturizer.

"Look at me, Shell," he pauses, giving me a moment to do as he asked. "You know how I feel about you. Why are you so reluctant to make this thing between us official? I'm just trying to love you and make you happy. Let me be there for you like you're there for everyone else. You deserve that, just… let me love you, woman!" He pleads, with sheer determination shining in his eyes.

I release a sigh. I guess it's time to put this beautiful man out of his misery. Not wanting to have this conversation naked, I grab my peach-colored Kaftan off the hook before walking over to my hot pink chase in the middle of the room to sit down.

"Rodney, no feelings, baby, that's what we agreed on, remember?" I express myself softly.

"Wait a minute Shell, that was…" he begins before I cut him off.

"No, you wait a minute, and just please.. just listen to what I have to say. Can you do that for me?"

Only after he nods his head do I continue. "We've been having a great time hanging out this past year. We like a lot of the same things, we're both career-driven, we love trying new exotic foods, and the sex... Well, it's actually life-altering." I mouth that part, throwing him a seductive wink, hoping to lighten his mood. "But relationships just aren't my thing, baby. I'm too set in my ways to change. You would end up miserable. I'm too selfish, self-centered, and extremely stubborn. On top of that, I love my living space way too much to share with anyone. I mean, I literally break out into hives if someone stays in my space for longer than ten days." I end with a chuckle because it is true.

I could see that he was still having a hard time with this, so I walked over and wrapped my arms around his waist. Craning my neck back to look up at him, I tell him, "I'm a mess, Rod. She destroyed my ability to let-" Before I can finish, he lets out a cold humorless laugh. "You're really going to stand here and tell me this tired ass shit." Dropping my arms to my sides, I follow him as he turns and walks back into my bedroom.

"You a real piece of work, you know that, Shell?" He asks while wagging a finger at me.

"Come now," I state, feeling my temperature begin to rise. "What we're not going to do is play the victim here. I made things perfectly clear, what I was looking for when we started this, did I not?"

He gives me one of those panty-drenching smiles while licking his lips. Causing an involuntary shudder to go through me. "Yeah, you made things perfectly clear, baby. You wanted me to come over here and blow your back out when you called. And after you cum real hard on the dick a few times, you want to send me on my merry way. Man, look," he says with frustra-tion. "Why not just hire a male escort or some shit?" He pauses as if he's waiting for an answer to that stupid ass question, so I obliged.

"Well, yeah... of course, I've ordered a male escort. Hell, a few times, if I'm being honest. One of the best decisions I've ever made because who has time for this bullshit!" I finished throwing my hands up.

For a while, we just stood there looking at each other. He finally lets out a low laugh, as he stuffed his hands in his pockets. Walking over to me, he bends down to place a soft kiss on my cheek. "You are an amazing woman Michelle Johnson..." I can tell he wanted to say more, but he decided against it. Turning toward the door, he not only walked out of my bedroom that night, but he also walked out of my life.

CHAPTER TWENTY-ONE

November 30th

Sam

LJ and Gio have become my very annoying and ever-present bodyguards. I know they mean well, but they're beginning to work my very last nerve. I groan, letting out a frustrated huff. I don't go anywhere without either one of them. I know it's out of concern, but I'm just tired of both of them at this point. Today, I've decided to invite LJ's guys over for lunch. LJ told me how concerned they all were about me. They sent me the most beautiful flowers. I wanted to do something nice in return and show them I was fine.

"You both better be on your best behavior." I say, glaring from LJ to Gio, "please don't make anyone feel uncomfortable ok?"

"I just don't understand why you have to do this so soon, Samantha," Gio says, his accent thick. Looking up at me from the sofa, his deep green eyes reflect every emotion he's feeling.

I go over to him, placing my hand on his cheek. I enjoy the

roughness of his beard against my skin. "It will all be fine, you'll see." I express, smiling down at him. It takes me by surprise when he cups my hand with his before he turns his head to place a tender kiss on the center of my palm. The sweet gesture made me blush. Instantly feeling self-conscious, I pulled my hand away and headed to the kitchen to make sure everything was ready.

Hearing the doorbell from the kitchen, I smile, knowing the guys have made it. I take a minute to get my emotions under control before I head out to greet everyone. Coming out of the kitchen, I see LJ, Cole, and Mason making their way inside. When they notice me in the doorway, everyone is quiet.

"Hi, fellas," I say brightly, walking over to them. Stopping in front of Mason, I ask, "how have you been? And, thank you for the beautiful flowers, Mason I..." Before I could finish, I was pulled into a strong hug. LJ and Gio, instantly on alert, move in our direction. I hold up my hand to stop them before placing it on Mason's back to comfort the gentle giant.

"I'm so sorry this happened to you, Ms. Sam. You're one of the sweetest people I know. You're always so kind to everyone and, and..."

I could tell he was at a loss for words, so I decided to rescue him.

"Why, thank you, Mason, I didn't know you cared," I tell him, making everyone laugh, successfully breaking the tension.

After lunch, I notice Cole standing off to the side, looking at our family pictures on the wall. Remembering LJ mentioned he had a family emergency a few weeks back, I decided to go over to talk to him.

"Hey, Cole, is everything ok?" I ask, smiling.

He turns to me, giving me his undivided attention. "Yes, everything's good. I'm so glad to see you up and about."

LJ told me Cole was there that day. I know he helped get me down the stairs and to the hospital.

"Cole, I wanted to thank you for helping LJ." I pause for a minute before continuing. "for helping me... that day."

I look down, too ashamed and embarrassed to continue.

"Come on, Sam. There's no need to thank me." He says, lifting my chin with his rough hand.

"We're family," he says with a smile that reaches those gorgeous blue eyes of his.

Pulling me into a hug, "I'm just relieved you and the baby are alright."

Instantly, I go still. I know everyone knows about the baby. They're all choosing not to talk about it for my benefit. Realizing I'm going to have to start talking about it sooner or later, I smile and thank him.

I know he's worried about me. They all are, I think to myself, looking around at these amazing men in my life. I truly appreciate each one of them at this moment. Unfortunately, Jay couldn't be here today, but he did send me a huge teddy bear with balloons.

See, just amazing men.

CHAPTER TWENTY-TWO

December 2

Sam

Monday morning, I'm up early to prepare for my busy day. I've already taken Killa for a nice long walk, made our breakfast—yes, I make his breakfast too; if I have a delicious breakfast, so is my fur baby—and took my vitamins. I'm now gathering my medical records to take to the police station. Feeling good, I headed out the door.

I can feel myself becoming angrier and frustrated by the second. I briefly close my eyes and draw in a couple of deep and calming breaths. I arrived at the police station around ten this morning. I informed the young man at the front desk that I wanted to speak with someone about a crime committed. After giving him my information, I was asked to have a seat. I smiled and thanked him for his help before I turned and anxiously did as he asked. While sitting there, I thought to myself, *"This is it!"* Hopefully, once the police open an active case, it won't take them too long to figure this mess out and prosecute whoever is responsible." Releasing a pent-up sigh, I feel more in control than I've felt in weeks. I sat there patiently and waited to be called.

About forty-five minutes later, a heavyset older white man in a wrinkled gray suit comes out and calls my name. I immediately got to my feet and followed him back into a small room with a table and two chairs. No sooner than we took our seats, I dove right in and explained everything I've remembered in great detail that has happened up until this point. I've laid out my doctor visits with Joann, medical records from the hospital, as well as the report LJ was given when the police came out to check the house. After I finish, I notice he's sporting a some-what comical expression on his face.

"This is a wild story, Mrs. Lane. It is Mrs, isn't it?

"Yes," I say.

"And you're saying it's not your husband's baby, right?"

"Correct," I slowly say, trying to understand where he's going with this.

"I see. I must be honest with you, Mrs. Lane." He says while rubbing the back of his neck. "I've heard stories like this before with women coming up with some pretty outlandish claims to get child support from some unsuspecting man. You'd be surprised by the stories a jilted lover can tell. And the sad part about it is a lot of these women have good loving husbands at home while they're out sleeping around with every Tom, Dick, and Harry."

As he continues to eye me, he asks? "How old did you say you were again, Mrs. Lane?

I sat there with my mouth open, unable to speak. "*No, this man didn't,*" I thought to myself in total disbelief. I'm having the hardest time trying to process what this man is not so subtly implying. He's boldly insinuating that I know who the father is, and I got pregnant on purpose to collect child support! He then goes on to ask my age. I assume he's trying to imply, a woman my age should know better; the nerve of this bastard!

Feeling my face heat, I know my eyes are as red as my vision right now.

"Look, I'm not trying to insult you, Mrs. Lane.

"It's a bit too late for that, officer," I spit out.

"Please try to see things from my point of view. You have no evidence to back up your claims. There's no evidence of rape or vaginal trauma anywhere in your chart. Your labs came back negative for Rohypnol, GHB, or Ketamine, the three most common date rape drugs that are sometimes present in crimes such as this. I do see here the "alleged crime" was committed over three months ago, so I'm a bit confused why the Dr. would waste resources by ordering a rape kit." He briefly looks up at me before clearing his throat and continues. "No forced entry into your home, so technically, there's been no crime committed." Leaning back in the chair, he crosses his arms over his round belly and says. "Now, I must ask you, Mrs. Lane, are you ready to give the name of the married man you're having an affair with behind your husband's back?" He finishes with a smug smile.

For a full minute, I sit there without blinking. Absently nodding my head, I realize I'd better leave right now. Moving quickly, I reach behind me to grab my purse off the chair. I stood up, gathering my things off the table. I do all this in silence because I know that if I don't get out of here right now, I'm going to jail for driving this pencil through this man's hand. This was a waste of my damn time, I think to myself, releasing a shaky breath. I will NOT break down in front of this asshole.

"I came here for help. I'm the victim! Officer Baldwin and I will be back." I state before turning and walking out the door.

CHAPTER TWENTY-THREE

Sam

I've been feeling hopeless and sorry for myself for the past two days. I woke up this morning finally feeling better. Pulling myself from the bed, I shuffle down the stairs and into the kitchen.

"Let's make mama a cup of tea, Killa. She needs it this morning," I murmured down to my fur baby at my feet. Moaning while going through the cabinets, searching for my favorite mug, I paused for a minute as a thought crossed my mind. "Hmm, what if there was someone out walking their dog or jogging that night that could have possibly seen something or someone." It's definitely worth looking into. Don't you think, baby? I glanced down, asking my partner in crime.

I pulled my lower lip between my teeth as I prop my hip against the counter. "Maybe I could put out flyers or," feeling movement from my cell momentarily pulls me from my thoughts. With a glance at the screen, a smile tugged at my lips.

"Good morning, Gio."

"Good morning, my dear Samantha. How are you feeling this morning?"

"I'm alive," I say under my breath with a chuckle.

"That's what I want to hear! Listen, pack a bag. I'm taking you away for a few days."

"What?! I can't go anywhere right now. I have to regroup and figure out my next move. Plus, I still haven't been able to reach Lance. I don't know why he's avoiding me. It's not like I'm going to just disappear. We're going to have to talk at some point. We still have to figure out what… wait, hold on, Gio, I have another call coming in."

"No problem, take your time, Sam." Came his patient reply.

"Hello?"

"Hi, is this Samantha Lane?" a cheery voice comes through the line.

"Um, Yes, this is Samantha Lane. How may I help you?" I answer, trying to place the voice.

"This is Gabriella Vargas. I'm Señor Chavez's assistant."

Not having a clue who Señor Chavez is, I reply, "Hi, Gabriella, how may I help you?"

I hear her soft chuckle come through the line before she says, "You're probably wondering why I'm calling?"

With a chuckle, I reply, "You would be correct. What can I do for you, Gabriella?"

"I'm calling on behalf of Señor Chavez, the owner of Diablo Salvaje distillery in Tequila Mexico.

My interest instantly peaked with the mention of tequila and Mexico in the same sentence. "I'm not familiar with Señor Chavez or his distillery, but please continue.

"Señor Chavez has heard so many wonderful things about you while away on a recent business trip. He was told about your tequila collection. That it's quite impressive, as well as extensive. Hearing about your love and appreciation for fine tequila has him intrigued. Once he heard how smart and beautiful you are, Señor Chavez decided he had to meet you."

Laughing a bit to mask my embarrassment, I clear my throat before slowly saying. "That's really sweet, Gabriella, but I'm not looking to entertain a suitor at this time."

"Oh, no, no! Ms. Lane, my apologies if you took that as a romantic meeting. Señor Chavez is happily married and has been for a very long time. In fact, the distillery got its infamous name from their love story. Diablo Salvaje means savage devil. That is what Señora Chavez's father called a young and very persistent Señor Chavez. Her father once said Señor Chavez was as relentless as a salvage devil in his pursuit for his young daughter's hand," she finishes, with a laugh. Señor Chavez was just so in awe after hearing about you. Hearing how dedicated and passionate you were when it comes to business and tequila. Is… is that still the case Ms. Lane? She finishes hesitantly.

I feel a little silly about jumping to conclusions, so I answer her. "Yes, that's still the case."

"That's great to hear! Señor Chavez hasn't come across many women that've shown as much interest in the tequila business as you. Especially one with your business background. He would like to speak with you about a few business matters and possibly your own tequila brand."

I'm in shock and left utterly speechless. I couldn't possibly have heard what I thought I just heard.

"Hello… Ms. Lane. Are you still there?"

After giving my head a quick shake, I'm finally able to reply. "Uh, yes, Gabriella, I'm here. I'm just in shock." I expressed a bit breathlessly.

"I totally understand," she says with a chuckle. "Señor Chavez would like to extend an invitation for you to come out to the Diablo Salvaje distillery in Tequila, Mexico. To experience the history of the distillery and tequila business in general. All of your expenses will be covered," I can hear the smile in her voice as she continues. "I believe you will enjoy your time here. It's really beautiful."

"Wow! I don't know what to say, and that rarely happens. "I say with a laugh as I try my hardest not to scream with excitement in the poor girl's ear. More calmly, I say, "All of this sounds lovely, truly a dream come true for me. Can I have your number to call you back once I've thought this over?"

"Of course! I will email you my contact information, with the itinerary attached. Please give me a call with your answer and any questions or concerns you may have. There's one last thing I wanted to mention. As a woman, I am personally excited for you to come out. This is an offer usually only extended to men, being that more men are interested in the tequila business. It's wonderful to see more women owning tequila brands. I also want to warn you that there will be quite a bit of tequila tasting. Señor Chavez is extremely proud of his family's tequila; he demands that everyone who tours the distillery learn the proper "Diablo Salvaje technique." for drinking tequila on the tour. Of course, it's all in fun. I hope that won't be a problem? I know it's silly for me to ask, being who you are, I just thought to mention it."

"Ah, no, not a problem at all." I answer absently," thank you for this call. It has definitely brightened my day. Please send that information over to me. You will be hearing from me in a day or so."

"Great! I'm looking forward to it."

"Oh, one last thing, Gabriella," I quickly say into the phone. "May I ask, who told Señor Chavez about me?" I already had an idea, I just needed her to confirm my suspicions.

"Yes, it was Giovanni Rossi. He spoke so highly of you. Señor Chavez was definitely impressed. That was sweet of him. You should thank him next time you see him.

"Yes, that was sweet of him, and I most certainly will thank him," I reply, smiling to myself, thinking of Gio. "I will talk to you soon, Gabriella. Thank you for calling, and enjoy the rest of your day."

"You, too, Ms. Lane. Bye for now." She says before hanging up.

"Oh my god, oh my god, oh my god!" I yelled out loud, "that couldn't have just happened." I ask, letting out a high-pitched squeal as I do a little dance. "Finally, some good news," I laugh.

"That must have been the call I was going to share with you on our way out of town."

I jump at the sound of a man's voice. "Gio?" I said into the phone, only now realizing I was still holding the phone to my ear.

"Yes, I'm still here," he says with laughter in his voice. "I take it you forgot you told me to hold on? Once you came back on the line, I didn't want to interrupt you from doing what I presume was your "happy dance," he says with a sexy laugh.

Finally getting my excitement under control and realizing what this man has done for me, I'm left speechless.

"Gio, thank-"

"Don't you dare thank me, Sam. I did nothing but tell an old man the truth. After I finished up a meeting with a potential client, I decided to go downstairs to the hotel bar and have a drink. I just so happened to sit down next to Señor Chavez. When I ordered a shot of tequila, he asked me what made me choose that particular brand. Being that you've schooled me so well on all things tequila, I turned to the man and told him about the story of Mrs. Samantha Lane, and the rest was history."

"Why, Gio? Why do you believe in me the way that you do?" I say with a trembling voice. "I'm... I'm broken." I finish in a whisper, too ashamed to say it any louder.

"Stop it, Samantha!" Came his sharp reprimand, "you are not broken; you are healing from something very traumatic. Also, it's past time for you to start seeing and believing in the amazing woman you are. Listen to me, all of this stress is just not good for you, and I want to remind you what it's like just to let loose and have a good time. Please don't deny one of your oldest and dearest friends Mia Bella. Please come away with me this weekend?

With that deep accented voice of his, he had me at hello.

Smiling while I playfully roll my eyes, I say, "Ok, ok, what time should I be ready?"

"That's what I wanted to hear! I'll pick you up at seven PM. Now go on and tell me about that call that had you squealing like a schoolgirl."

Unable to contain my excitement, I did just that for the next thirty minutes. Gio being Gio, listened and hyped me up as only a true friend could.

CHAPTER TWENTY-FOUR

Sam

Hearing my doorbell ring, I glanced up at the clock. As I expected, seven o'clock on the dot. You can always count on Gio to be punctual. I giggle to myself, heading over to answer it.

I opened the door with a flourish. I couldn't help but smile while taking him in. "Why Giovanni, don't you look nice" I say as I finish checking him out with appreciation. Gio really is a gorgeous man. It took me a while, but I finally felt comfortable being around him. With his devilish good looks, I always felt even more nervous and self-conscious about my weight whenever he was around. I'm not sure if he was even aware of this. If he was, I appreciated that he never brought it up. I was kind of a loner in college. He changed that the day I met him and Lance.

Ruby, my college roommate, was very outgoing and loved to party. She often tried to convince me to go out with her and her friends. That was something that was never going to happen, but I appreciated her thinking of me. They were all super nice, but I knew that I didn't fit in with them. *Not one of them heffas was plagued by the dreaded freshman fifteen. Unfortunately for me, I picked up those fifteen and then some on my already fuller frame. I would always thank her for the invite before I'd politely refuse.*

One Saturday afternoon, while lying across my bed reading, I could hear Ruby's wails before she made it into our room. Coming through the door, my gorgeous roommate's face was bright red with tears.

"He broke up with me, Sam! I've done nothing but love and support him for the past two years, and he breaks up with me?" She finished before throwing herself into my arms.

Kevin, Ruby's on-again, off-again boyfriend was a real asshole. It didn't surprise me that he was playing those games again. Whenever he came by, he always found a way to "accidentally" rub my ass. Wanting to take her mind off of him, I leaned back, pulled her beautiful face in my hands, and said, "let's go get drunk."

Through her pain, she was able to register what I was saying and squealed! "Ooh ooh ooh, I know the perfect place."

Fifteen minutes later, we pulled up in front of a little hole in the wall bar. I don't think I would have even known it was there if not for Ruby. Opening the door, the dim interior was momentarily flooded with sunlight. Once inside, we spotted a table with two chairs near the back.

"What would you like to start with?" I asked my friend, hoping to cheer her up.

"Anything that would make me forget the last two years I wasted on that asshole," she pitifully said.

"I got you," I replied before heading over to the bar.

"Excuse me, what drink do you recommend for a broken heart?" I asked the older bartender, who smiled sympathetically at me while cleaning glasses.

A couple of hours and three tequila shots later, I was having the time of my life when the door opened, bathing the small bar in sunlight once again. I absently looked over my shoulder to see two men walk in. As they made their way further inside, my eyes adjusted to see two of the most beautiful men I've ever seen. With the tequila giving me liquid courage, I boldly took them in one at a time. They both stood around 6'2 or 6'3. One had the most delicious dark chocolate skin. He sported a muscular, athletic frame, a bald head with thick sensual lips.

As my eyes slid from "Mr. good bar," I took my time taking in "Mr. tall, dark and handsome." I noticed his shoulders were a bit broader than his friend's. He had an olive complexion, black wavy hair tucked behind his ears, and beautiful green eyes. As I pulled my lower lip between my teeth, a nasty thought crossed my mind. "He would definitely be able to handle all this," I was instantly shocked. Where the hell did that come from? Clearly, I'm not either one of their types. Sighing, I dropped my gaze and turned back around.

'Girl, you see something you like?" Ruby giggled.

As I was about to reply, I heard a deep sexy voice. "Excuse me?" I turned to see Mr. "tall, dark, and handsome" standing behind me. I drew in a breath as I stared into those gorgeous green eyes fanned by the longest lashes I'd ever seen on a man. Even with the dim light, I was still able to get a good look at them.

As I continued to gaze up at him, I heard Ruby laugh and say. "mm, Sam, he's waiting for you to reply."

Instantly snapping out of my trance, I felt my face heat up as I asked, "Can I help you?"

"My grandfather once told me when a woman holds eye contact, it's as if she's summoning you over to say hello."

"Really?" I say a bit breathlessly, loving the sound of his voice. "Where's your grandfather from?"

"Italy. I'm Giovanni, but everyone calls me Gio." He offers.

I accepted his warm outstretched hand, and I told him. "I'm Samantha, but everyone calls me Sam." unable to stop the smile that played on my lips.

"I really should feel some type of way about you abandoning me,

man. You invited me to go have a drink, remember?" I heard from behind Gio. As Mr. Good bar approached us, he introduced himself as well. "Hello, beautiful, I'm Lance, and you are?" He finished with his hand extended.

Instantly on guard with the "beautiful endearment, "I'm Sam." I said while shaking his hand a bit more reserved. This is my friend Ruby." I gestured to the tortured beauty across from me.

"Are you both students at Cal Gio asks?"

Nodding, I give a small smile.

"I can't believe I've never run into you." He must have noticed my discomfort because he quickly added, "either of you on campus." He finished shifting his eyes between me and Ruby with a warm smile.

"We sure haven't," Lance said to me, rubbing his hands together and flashing that drop-dead gorgeous smile of his. "But with all the girls chasing this one around campus," he said, gesturing to Gio with his thumb, "he wouldn't notice his own mother," he laughed, causing Gio to give him an irritated glance.

After looking around the bar, Gio's gaze returned to mine before asking if it was alright for them to join us. Ruby's enthusiastic "yes!" answered for both of us. As they slid another table up to ours, I got a better look at them both. Yep, Just as I suspected... both were very nice but way out of my league.

I learned two things about that memorable day, one: I loved tequila, and two: that was the day that would change my life forever

From that moment on, Gio Lance and I became inseparable. Ruby and Kevin eventually got back together, so she was rarely around anymore. The three of us would talk for hours about starting a business. Being that I was a business major and Lance and Gio architecture majors, we formed GLS construction enterprise. The plan was to build commercial buildings across the country. Gio always made me feel comfortable in my own skin, never suggesting we go to the gym or automatically ordering me a salad and diet drink when we all went out for a bite to eat like Lance. I always felt that Gio and I had a *connection that Lance and I never did. I remember thinking, If only I could ever build enough courage, I would ask Gio out on a date. I think they both started to pick up on my little crush. That's why I was so confused that night when Lance showed up at my dorm room right before winter break...*

CHAPTER TWENTY-FIVE

Sam

While riding along the California coast, with the top down in Gio's beautiful Mercedes Benz S-Class, I felt alive. Feeling the sun shining on my face and the wind blowing through my hair, I truly felt free with no cares in the world. I have absolutely no idea where we're headed. He told me he wanted it to be a surprise. I don't quite know how I feel about that, being in the dark. This is something very new for me. I'm the one that made all the reservations, so I always knew where we were going. I sigh as another thought hits me. I was also the one that packed our bags and made sure Lance's schedule was clear. All Lance ever had to do was show up. Deciding to leave those memories alone, I allow my mind to drift to more pleasant ones.

"We've arrived, Mia Bella." I hear Gio murmur into my ear. Opening my eyes slowly, I look around to take in my surroundings.

Once I realize where we are, I snap to a sitting position and grab for his arm. "Oh my god, Gio! we're staying at the Cliff Resort?!" I can't help but squeal.

All he does is smile. He knows how much I love this place and what it means to me. The Cliff Resort is simply breathtaking. Some of our out-of-state clients that come into the office, always ask about places to visit, while they're here in California. I always recommend The Cliff Resort. Even though I've never stayed there myself, it truly is a beautiful hotel that sits nestled on a cliff overlooking the Pacific Ocean. We've passed through Pismo Beach many times, traveling from Northern California down to Southern California for business. With our schedules packed tight, we would normally only stop in for a brief lunch, or dinner in the hotel's restaurant.

On one of those trips, after we had dinner, Lance and Gio stopped to speak with an acquaintance at the bar. I took that time to stretch my legs and walked around the hotel. I found a small trail out back that led to a cliff, overlooking the ocean. I listened to the waves crashing against the rocks down below while gazing out at the setting sun's reflection on the still water. It was breathtaking and filled me with peace. Hearing someone behind me, I glance over my shoulder to see Gio approaching. I remember closing my eyes and breathing in as much of the salty air my lungs could hold. Releasing it, I told him, once business calms down and Lance could manage for a few days without me, I wanted to come here and stay a few days. Maybe get a massage and tour the area. I remember the thoughtful expression that crossed his handsome face before he replied, "That sounds lovely, Samantha. You, of all people, deserve it." We stood there in silence, taking in the beautiful sight until Lance came to tell us it was time to go.

I turned to Gio with tears in my eyes, "Thank you, Gio, thank you for this. This is one of the best surprises I've ever had!" I say with trembling lips. I swear these pregnancy hormones have me happy and sad at the same time.

"Stop, Samantha. You deserve this and so much more." He finishes, looking deep into my eyes. With a wicked grin, he says, "let us go get checked in so we can start having some fun," he finishes while wiggling his eyebrows.

I can't help but laugh. I couldn't make it out of the damn car fast enough. I am ready. Let the fun begin.

Sunday morning, I wake up relaxed and well-rested. Sitting up in bed, I raise my arms high above my head and bend into a nice long stretch. We really have had a ball these past few days. Every morning we would wake to begin a new adventure. We'd start each day with a light breakfast before setting out to explore. I was overjoyed we were able to visit the Monarch Butterfly grove. I've loved butterflies my whole life. I remember my sisters and I used to run through a field full of butterflies behind my grandma Hattie's house. I'd stare in amazement at their bright, colorful wings. I would let my head fall back while watching butterflies, from the size of the pad of my index finger to the size of my entire hand flying above. I would always hold out my hand and wish that one would bless me by landing on it. So, when Gio told me that's where we were headed, I could barely contain my excitement. I had to promise him I wouldn't embarrass either one of us once we got inside. I think with a chuckle.

I learned some pretty interesting things about Monarch butterflies. Like, they gather in basketball clusters to sleep, and they are unable to fly if it is below fifty-five degrees Fahrenheit. I loved every minute of that tour. The next day, I had a little surprise of my own, set up for Gio. Like tequila is my passion, wine is his. So, that day was all about wine. We toured small family-owned wineries to some of the larger well-known ones. We decided to skip the wine tasting, due to obvious reasons, and went shopping instead. I made sure to pick up some bottles of wine for Gio's parents, as well as for my bestie. Walking along the Pismo Beach Pier, we dined on delicious gourmet street food and talked for hours. I'm so happy I allowed myself to just live in the moment. My mind instantly wanders back to that tangy sauce I couldn't get enough of yesterday. Usually, I would have just ordered a chicken salad or something light on vacation. Not wanting to consume too many calories. Lance would have never...

"Nope, not today, Samantha," I murmured to myself, cutting off that line of thinking. Finally getting out of bed, I head into the bathroom. Coming out, I'm showered and dressed for the day. I almost skip over to my phone to see what adventures Gio has planned for us. To my surprise, I have a message from The Cliff Resort Full Spectrum Spa. Opening the message, it's a reminder for an eleven AM sixty-minute prenatal massage scheduled for this morning. I sat on the bed speechless. Feeling my phone vibrate, I look down to see Gio's name on the screen. Smiling, I answer.

"Good morning, Giovanni."

"Good morning, my dearest Samantha. I'm sure you're aware by now of your very important appointment that awaits. I will be at your door in approximately twenty seconds to escort you downstairs. I suggest you hurry that delectable ass of yours so that you won't be late."

Laughing, I hang up and do as he asked.

As we reached the lobby, Gio pointed me in the direction of the spa. He placed a soft kiss on my cheek before telling me he would see me in an hour. Walking inside, I'm greeted with a warm smile by the friendly receptionist. Looking at her, I can't help but smile. She kinda reminds me of Dolly Parton in the movie 9 to 5. That was one of my favorite movies. I love Dolly Parton!

"You must be Samantha?" she asks with a bright smile that lights up her eyes.

"Yes, I am. Good morning!" I cheerfully say, smiling at the friendly reception.

"You've already been cleared for the prenatal massage by your O.B." Briefly, she glances down at her notes before saying, "Dr. Joann, I believe?"

"Yes!" I reply in disbelief.

She smiled at my shock, and she told me, "you've got yourself a wonderful fella there. He thought of everything. He called us a couple of days before you both arrived, to see what was needed for the massage. He's very thorough." She finishes.

"That he surely is," I say with a soft laugh.

"Please have a seat, and make yourself comfortable. Cindy will be out to get you shortly."

As I walked over to the ultra-plush waiting area, I couldn't remove the silly little grin I know I'm sporting if I tried.

After that wonderful massage, Gio and I had a light lunch before parting ways for the afternoon. I had a couple of business calls I needed to make, as well as a few emails that needed to be sent. We have a dinner reservation at seven PM. Therefore, I didn't waste any time getting to work once I got back to my room. The first order of business was sending Gabriella an email, letting her know I accepted Señor Chavez's generous offer. I informed her the week of January fourteenth works for me. She replied instantly, letting me know she would send everything I needed for the trip. After that, I worked on a few things that needed my attention. A couple of hours later, I let out a big yawn. Standing up and stretching, I put my laptop away, deciding to take a quick nap before dinner.

Looking at the clock, I see that it's 7:11 PM. I frown, thinking, *"This is so unlike Gio to be late."* A Thought comes to me, making me giddy with excitement, *"I will surprise him this evening by picking him up for dinner instead."* I cleverly think, with a mischievous grin on my lips. I took my time getting ready this evening. I decided to wear my DVF leopard print, wrap dress.

Lance always hated this dress, so I didn't wear it often, but I love it. Tonight, I decided not to hide my curves but show them off a little. I smile as I take in my side reflection. I do have a baby bump now, but my large breasts help camouflage it. I realized, laughing to myself. After putting the finishing touches on my makeup, I slide my freshly pedicured feet into my black patent leather peep-toe Christian Louboutin heels and head out the door.

His room is only a couple of doors down from mine, so I didn't have to walk very far. Excited to see him, I raised my hand, then hesitated. *What if he had company? He could have met some gorgeous woman today in the hotel bar and invited her up to his room.* Biting my lower lip, as my smile slides from my lips, my mind wanders to Lance's parting words. *"You're a fat forty-five yr old single mother, who's going to want you."* Sighing, I lower my hand and decide to go back to my room. As soon as I step away from the door, it opens, and Gio steps out.

"Good, you're here!" He exclaims excitedly. "I was on my way to get you." Pausing, a slow smile spreads across his face as he takes me in. "Why, don't you look ravishing tonight, Samantha." He says, leaning in to place a soft kiss on my cheek. "Do you mind coming in? I would like to show you something?"

I smile and nod yes, trying my best to shake off the melancholy. Once I step into his room, a soft gasp leaves my lips. Out on the balcony, there's a beautifully set table for two. Soft candlelight illuminates the room as soft music plays in the background.

"Sorry, I'm late. It took a little longer than expected." He says from behind me.

"It's our last night here. I thought maybe we could have dinner here, overlooking the ocean." He says with a smile.

"Everything's so beautiful, Gio!" I tell him, with my hands over my mouth. "Thank you for all of this," I say a bit breathlessly as I turn around, taking everything in.

He smiles, grabbing my hand and bringing it to his lips. "Come, Mia Bella, let's go eat."

While eating, we laugh and reminisce about our college days. After a while, I notice Gio grows quiet.

"Samantha, I have to share something with you."

Placing my knife and fork down, I wipe my mouth with my napkin before giving him my undivided attention.

"I'm in love with you, Sam. I always have been and always will be. I... I know you may be thinking this is a shitty thing to say to my best friend's wife. You have to understand that I've loved you from the moment I met you. I didn't want to rush things with you in college, I wanted you to get to know me first. I didn't want you to think that I was a womanizer or was only trying to sleep with you. When I started to notice you taking an interest in me, I told Lance. I let him know that I was finally going to ask you out when we all returned to school from winter break. He knew I had genuine feelings for you from the start, Samantha" he pauses with deep hurt swimming in his eyes. Looking down, he finishes, "But of course, when I got back to school, everything had changed...

Sam

The night before I was to head home for winter break, Lance came to my dorm room. He had just learned his beloved family dog had passed away and was beside himself with grief. Dropping to his knees in front of me, he placed his head in my lap and cried his heart out. I don't know how long we stayed like that, with me rubbing his back, trying to provide him comfort as best I could. At one point, Lance raised his head and stared into my eyes. Slowly, he grabbed my face in his hands and kissed me. Shocked, I try to pull back and tell him this isn't what he needed. Taking advantage of my parted lips, he thrust his tongue into my mouth, kissing me so thoroughly I was breathless when we parted. Getting to his feet, he took my hand, pulling me up into a tight hug. Silently, we stayed like that as I watched the bright moon-

shine through my window. I remember praying that I was giving him the comfort he desired.

He leaned back, looked into my eyes, and asked, "do you want this?" I barely heard him say as I looked up at him with confused eyes.

He cleared his throat and asked a bit louder, "do you want this, Sam?"

I remember thinking, I've never seen Lance like this, so vulnerable, so open. Biting my lip nervously, taking in a shaky breath, I looked up into his eyes, nodding my head yes, yes—I wanted this.

When we all arrived back at school, Lance and I was officially a couple.

"I was devastated to learn that you and Lance were together. After that day, I decided I just wanted you to be happy, and I would try to be content with sharing your life from the sidelines. I wanted the best for both of you, I did. But I knew deep down if the opportunity ever presented itself, especially with lance being..." Gio pauses, before continuing, "if the opportunity ever presented itself, I would take it and worship the ground you walk on until my dying day. I know things are complicated right now, Samantha," he says while taking my hand in his. "I want you to know I'm here for as long as you want me to be. I am not going anywhere. Ok?"

I couldn't help smiling brightly at this beautiful man. I nodded my head and said. "ok."

That night, I slept in Gio's room. We didn't have sex. We both knew there was time for that, plus what we did was so much more special to me. We laughed, talked, and just connected on so many levels.

As I laughed at something funny Gio just shared, I was caught off guard by a big yawn.

"I'm sorry, I haven't stayed up this late in a long time," I said bashfully.

He smiles and sets his glass down on the table. After he stood, he extended his hand to help me to my feet. Leading me into the bedroom, he walked over to the bed and had me sit down. Going down on his knee, he begins removing my shoes. After removing his own, he climbed onto the bed before pulling my body close to his. I closed my eyes and snuggled back into him. I felt something I hadn't experienced in a very long time, Intimacy.

CHAPTER TWENTY-SIX

Sam

As we're pulling up to the house, I see LJ playing fetch outside with Killa. Seeing my boys brings a smile immediately to my face. Barely opening my door, Killa is the first one to the car to welcome me home.

"Did you miss mama?" I ask while swooping him up into my arms. "Boy, stop moving before I drop you." I laugh, having to get a better grip on him before his excited body falls out of my hands.

"Hey, Ma! Don't you look well-rested." LJ beams, leaning in to give me a peck on the cheek.

"Hey, my Sonshine! Have you been out here long?"

"Naw, Jay just left, he stopped by for a minute. I had him help me pull your packages into the garage."

"Packages?" Tilting my head to the side, I ask. "What packages, honey?"

I look in the direction he is pointing as he says, "When I got here this afternoon, three large boxes had been delivered in front of the garage. I figured you ordered some new furniture." He finishes, trying to gauge my reaction.

"Huh, that's odd," I say while shaking my head, "I don't believe I ordered anything, but you know your mama." Curiosity getting the best of me, I went to open the garage. With LJ, and Gio instantly at my side, I try to see if there are any pictures on the boxes. I turn one around as my shaking hands fly to cover my mouth. It's a brand new crib! I look at the pictures on the other boxes to see a stroller and mattress for the crib. "What the hell?" I mumbled through my quaking hands.

I can feel my chest begin to rise and fall at a rapid pace. I try hard not to overreact. I can hear LJ on the phone with Shell, asking if she sent them. *Please let this be from Shell.* I pray under my breath, with my eyes closed. But I have a sinking feeling that it's not.

"Naw Ma," LJ says, hanging up the phone. "Aunt Shell said she didn't send them.

"It's him! I know this is all from him." I scream, looking everywhere but seeing nothing. I feel Gio's strong arms pull me to him. I turn and cry into his chest. "What does he want, Gio? Why is he doing this to me?" I freeze as a scary thought occurs to me. "Oh no," I whisper with wide eyes, "He's coming for the baby! I have to move." I say, looking around frantically, trying to figure out where to start.

"Samantha! You have got to calm down! This isn't good for you or the baby." Gio says firmly, holding onto my arms and looking into my wide eyes. "I swear to you, on my life, I won't let anything happen to you or the baby. He continues to hold me in his fierce stare until I nod that I hear him.

"Come on, mama, let's get you inside," LJ says as he gently guides me into the house.

All that keeps running through my mind is that he's somewhere watching and waiting. But for what? What could he possibly want from me?

CHAPTER TWENTY-SEVEN

Sam

Thursday afternoon, I'm sitting in front of the Marriott hotel, trying to summon the courage to get out of the car. Lance has refused to take any of my calls. I have tried to be patient with this man, but it's well past time for us to talk. It wasn't difficult for me to find out where he was staying. LJ gave me the information a couple of weeks back. I was hoping Lance would come to his senses before I had to ambush him. Sighing, I look at my reflection in the rearview mirror one last time before getting out of the car. I know he's not going to be too happy about me just showing up like this, but he's given me no other option. We have more than our current dilemma to talk about. We still own a thriving, high-functioning business together that needs to be discussed. Gio has been pulling every-one's weight, and it's time for that to stop. I don't want to argue with him. I just want to start the conversation. Gathering my courage, I head towards the hotel's entrance. On the elevator, I close my eyes and take deep breaths as it carries me up to the eleventh floor. I jump slightly, hearing the elevator ding. As the doors slide open, I step out on unsteady legs.

I closed my eyes and tried to steady my breathing. "Come on, Samantha, you can do this," I whisper under my breath. Taking a final cleansing breath, I look down at the paper for the room number. Seeing that it's to my left, I turn and head in that direction. I know the room should be just around the bend. I slow down, hearing voices up ahead. One, in particular, gives me pause. That's Lance! I would know the sound of his voice anywhere. I slowly peer around the bend and gasp my hands fly to my mouth. Lance is standing slightly in the hall, in nothing but a pair of black boxers, his arms wrapped tightly around a woman. I didn't need to see her face to know who it was. Cassie, I would know those scarlet dreadlocks anywhere.

"Call me as soon as you make it home, baby. He says before kissing her passionately.

"I will, baby." Came Cassie's soft reply. If I had any doubts about who this woman was before, her next words confirmed her identity. She told him she planned to have dinner with Shell this evening, and she'd probably be back late.

Not wanting to be seen, I quickly head back the way I came. Thank god the elevator was still on the floor. I hurriedly pressed the button, and the doors instantly opened for me. With my Panic still riding me, I rushed inside and repeatedly pressed the down button simultaneously with the button to close the doors. I quickly glanced outside to see if anyone was there. Only when the elevator began to move did I let out a sigh of relief. Leaning heavily against the mirrored elevator wall. So many things run through my mind at once. The one that I'm having the hardest time wrapping my head around is that Lance is having an affair with my best friend's little sister.

Later that night, I lie in bed thinking about this Lance and Cassie situation. To say I'm shocked is truly an understatement. Releasing a heavy sigh, I realize I don't know what I'm going to do about it just yet. So I decided to leave it for another day. I turned my lamp off and tried to get some sleep...

That night, I had the weirdest dream.

Rough, calloused hands all over my body... soft lips pressing into my spine... releasing a soft moan, as my legs are spread wide... Feeling a hand caress my face... I briefly open my eyes to see blue or maybe green eyes staring back into mine, almost lovingly...

The next morning, I woke up with an uneasy feeling in the pit of my stomach. Trying to wrap my head around that dream, I slam my fists down on the bed and scream. There's just so much happening at once that I feel like I'm losing my mind. Breathing heavily, I bow my head. "I can't handle all of this," I whisper brokenly. I can't go through life fearing someone going to jump out at any given moment. Dropping my head in my hands I start breathing deeply, trying to calm myself. "Get it together, Samantha, get it together, girl." I chastise myself out loud. I have to figure out a way to keep me and this baby safe, but how? Feeling hopeless, I lower my head and allow the tears to fall...

CHAPTER TWENTY-EIGHT

Sam

I'm sitting in Joann's waiting room for my monthly prenatal appointment, feeling even more confused and rattled, *if that's even possible*, after that dream. Trying to relieve the pressure in my head, I massage my temples with my eyes closed. Gio and LJ both wanted to be here but had important meetings at work this morning. I assured them I was fine to come alone. They only agreed after I promised I would call them after with updates. Trying to think of anything other than my current situation, I looked around at the few pregnant women also waiting. Pulling out my phone, I pull up Pinterest trying to get nursery ideas.

"Do you mind if I sit here?" I hear a quiet voice say.

I look up to see a very pregnant young woman. Smiling warmly, "Of course you can." I said, gesturing to the seat beside me. As she sits, she lets out a rough sigh. I notice she's really pretty and very young. She puts me in the mind of Molly Ringwald, with her short red hair and cute pink lips. "Are you ok? Would you like for me to get you some water?" I offer.

"That's very kind of you, but no, thank you." She says with a small smile.

"Smiling back, "I'm Sam," I tell her.

"Celeste," she replies. "Are you here waiting on your daughter?" she innocently asks.

I close my eyes, breathing in and releasing it before smiling. "Nope, I'm here for me," I tell her, patting my fleshy stomach.

"I am so sorry!" she begins with wide eyes, "I didn't mean to offend you."

I held up my hand to halt her apology I smiled and let her know it was alright.

I definitely understand her reaction. I probably would have drawn the same conclusion. To put the young woman at ease, I ask her, "how far along are you?"

"Almost eight months," she replies.

"Wow! Almost there, "has it been an easy pregnancy?"

She sighs while shaking her head No, causing those pretty red curls to frame her face.

"Do you want to talk about it?" I softly ask.

"I made a stupid mistake, I believed David really loved me, but once I told him I was pregnant, he was gone. All I have is my grandmother. She has been amazing through all of this. She took me in when she could have just as easily turned me away. She's helped me so much already with buying things to prepare for the baby." She takes a breath before she continues.

She points over to the front desk and says, "The lady just told me that I missed the registration deadline to receive a free car seat this clinic gives out. I was counting on getting one of those because we don't have much money for the larger baby items'." she finishes with a dejected look covering her face.

My heart goes out to the young mother, so I decide to help.

"Oh, yeah, I vaguely remember the receptionist telling me she signed me up to receive something. How about I give you mine?" I simply say. "You know what, I also have a brand new crib, and stroller you are welcomed to have." I finish, giving her a bright smile.

With wide brown eyes, Celeste begins shaking her head. "I couldn't possibly accept that, you... you need that stuff for your baby!" she exclaims while gesturing toward my stomach.

I wasn't about to tell her. There was no way in hell my baby would ever use that stuff. So instead, I told her I ordered those things before realizing they were the wrong color, and I would have to buy them again anyway.

Not able to contain her happiness, she grabs me and pulls me into an awkward hug. Laughing, I pat her back, telling her she's welcome.

On my way home from my appointment, I made sure to stop at Babies R Us to buy a car seat with a couple more baby items to ship with the crib and stroller.

After I pulled into my driveway, I just sat there for a while, with my head against the headrest. I finally had time to think over Lance's betrayal. "I wonder if he did this to get back at me. He knows how close Shell and I are. She and Cassie are like family to me.

"Alexa, call Michelle," I say out loud. Hearing the phone begin to ring, as I let out a shaky sigh, I'm not sure why I'm so nervous to tell her what's been happening.

"Hey, girl." She answers in that chipper voice of hers.

"Hey, Shell, how's your day going?"

"Good, girl. No scratch that, it's great! We just closed on a large commercial property that's been giving me hell, but I got it." She finishes laughing.

"That's great! We have to celebrate!"

"Yes, we do. Now, what's up, girl? You never call me in the middle of the day, everything ok? How are you and the little nugget?" She asks with concern.

"Everything's good, but I need to tell you something." Letting out a sigh, I told her everything I saw that day I went to Lance's hotel. After I had finished, I was met with silence.

"Shell, are you still there?"

"Look, Sam," she says, releasing a frustrated sigh before continuing. I don't know what you may have thought you saw, but, I can assure you, Cassie would never do something like that!"

"Shell."

"No, Sam, let me finish. I've always tried to be there for you, no matter how needy you were, but I must say, your low self-esteem is beginning to affect your judgment." She says before hanging up the phone.

Staring at the console with my mouth open, all I can think is what in the hell just happened.

CHAPTER TWENTY-NINE

Sam

The next morning, I woke up feeling surprisingly well-rested, considering what happened with Shell. Thinking about my friend, I realize I am not mad. Maybe a little hurt, hearing her say those awful things, but I get it. I really do. I also know how devastated she's going to be once everything settles, and we will get through it. "But not this week!" I say out loud. Realizing my trip to Mexico is coming up. I didn't know how excited I was about this trip until this very moment. Grabbing my laptop, I head to the kitchen to eat and tie up any remaining business.

The last few days have been utter chaos trying to get everything in order. I started the day with an early morning appointment with Joann to get my clearance to travel. After that, I rushed home to give my house a thorough cleaning before settling down to pack. "What are you forgetting, Sam?" I ask myself looking around my room. Right at that moment, I hear LJ's horn outside. "Shit, he's here already?" I say out loud, hurrying towards the door. Grabbing my purse off the sofa and Killa at my feet, I rushed out the front door.

"Hey, Sonshine," I say to him before leaning over to pop a kiss on his cheek. "Thanks for doing this for me. Are you sure it won't be a problem staying here for the week with Killa?"

He returns the kiss on my cheek before saying, "Of course it's not a problem, Ma. I told you, me, and Gio got this, so no worries." He pauses while glancing over at me. "I just want you to try to relax and enjoy yourself, ok?"

"I will, son, but you do know this is a business trip, right?"

"I know. Just promise me that you will try to let your hair down and relax, alright?"

"I will, baby, I promise," I finish, giving a big cheesy grin. After that, I settle back as he takes me around to do my last-minute errands before my flight in the morning. Feeling my cell vibrate, I look down to see a message from Gio.

Gio: See you bright and early in the morning, beautiful. I wish I was going with you.

Me: Me too! Are you sure you can't come? Can it be another getaway for us?

Gio: someone has to be here and keep the business thriving, I'm still unable to reach Lance, so I'm pretty much in the office around the clock. But I will be there to take you to the airport in the morning, my love.

Me: Thank you, baby, you're just too good to me.

I looked up to see we were almost at my sister Eboni's hair salon. I have a two PM. appointment for French braids with one of her hair technicians. I'm so proud of my baby sister, I think while smiling from ear to ear. When she first came to me fresh out of cosmetology school and wanted me to invest in her hair salon, I said no. Eboni hadn't been known to stick to anything long-term. Front a job, a boyfriend, or not even a place to live. She gets bored easily and has to shake up the scenery from time to time, as she says.

Instead, I made a deal with her. If she finds a salon to work at and stays there for one year, we could revisit this conversation. Not only did the girl rise to the challenge, but she also surprised me by saving a little nest egg for her business. That really blew my mind because Eboni usually spends every dollar she gets her hands on.

Eboni did everything I asked, so me and Shell worked our magic and found her a small building in a nice location. This turned out to be one of the best investments I've ever made. Eboni shocked me once again with her business savvy. We recently sat down to talk about possibly expanding and adding another location. She came to me well prepared, I think back with pride. I remember her walking into my office in her business attire and game face on.

We pulled in front of a pretty white building with a large bay window that read, *"The Beauty of It, Hair Chateau"* in gold elegant letters on it.

"Ok, Ma, me and Killa are going to run to my place to pick up my stuff. Call me when you're ready."

Getting out of the car, I grab my purse and romance novel before heading inside.

"Ok, Samantha, time for a change," I say to myself as I walk into the lavish building.

CHAPTER THIRTY

Sam

I'm so happy I decided to get my hair braided at the last minute, I think as I toss a few of them over my shoulder. The last thing I needed was to deal with my hair in this sweltering heat. A small smile plays across my lip as Gio crosses my mind. He made sure I was at the airport yesterday morning, bright and early, with time to spare. Opening my front door, I was met with a kiss and a cup of my favorite coffee. *He's so thoughtful.* I thought to myself right before the smile slid from my lips when he mentioned Lance's name. He told me they talked and decided to meet up for dinner tomorrow night. I nibbled on my lower lip before asking if he was planning to tell him about us. Gio, being Gio, replied, "What kind of question is that? Of course, I'm planning to tell him and anyone that will listen. You, my love, belong to me now." He declares with mischief gleaming in his eyes. "I would gladly shout it from the rooftops, Samantha." Grabbing my hand, he brings it to his lips. "You are my greatest blessing. I plan to cherish you for the rest of my life." After that, the only thing I could do was say, "ok," with a silly grin.

Walking downstairs, I can't help but marvel at how beautiful this staircase is. I think while running my hand across the intricate details of the handrail. Señor Chavez and his beautiful wife insisted I stay with them in their beautiful home. It is a spectacular hacienda-style villa with vibrant artwork throughout the beautiful space. Inspired by the old Mexican haciendas of the eighteenth century, I was told. While taking my time getting ready this morning, I have to remind myself that this is a business trip and not a fabulous vacation. The outfit I chose to wear today was a white tank top tucked into a pair of, white wide-leg pants. At first, I wasn't too sure if I would even be able to pull off this look with my ever-growing belly, but I made it work. I tied the look together with my black Gucci 1955 Horsebit wallet chain with a pair of black Gucci sandals to adorn my feet. My large print, black and white kimono flows behind me as I make my way downstairs. Having larger breasts, they're hard to hide, so I decided to showcase them in a classy, sophisticated way. I wore my wide gold cuff bracelets on my wrists with gold hoop earrings. I decided to compliment my black and white outfit with a bold red lip. Feeling kind of cute, I decided to take a few selfies for Instagram.

As I stepped outside, I noticed the amazing gardens with all the beautiful flowers and palm trees. A gentle breeze picks up, carrying the most amazing scent provided by the array of bold, colorful flowers. I close my eyes, breathing in the aromatic arrangement. I've always loved the light and fresh scent of morning dew. The flowers gave it a sweeter note this morning. Walking out further, I looked around for someone to bother with, taking a few pictures for me. While looking, I decided to take a stroll and marvel at the beauty of this place. I noticed the beautiful hand-carved metalwork and natural stone finishes throughout this villa. Making my way to the other side, I see two young women taking pictures by a beautiful water fountain. "I'm in luck," I sing to myself as I hurry over to them. "Disculpe, ¿puede tomarme una foto, por favor?"

"Sure!" The pretty brunette says in English, waving me over.

"Thank you!" I say with a grateful sigh. My Spanish is far from fluent, but I do like to practice with native speakers whenever I can.

I handed her my iPhone and over near the beautiful fountain to strike a pose.

"No, no, you can do better than that!" she says, chuckling, "Monica, go show her how it's done." She waves over to the other woman. After my impromptu photoshoot, I'm looking at my photos in awe.

Shaking my head in disbelief, I tell her, "these are great; thank you! Are you a photographer?"

She blushed beautifully while shaking her head.

"Well, you should be, these are fabulous! My best friend is going to be so jealous when she sees these." I squeal as I go through the photos.

"You are welcome, Señora, glad we could help. You look beautiful, by the way." She smiles before heading inside.

I sat on the edge of the water fountain for a few minutes to post pictures on Facebook and Instagram. I instantly get a text from Gio, making me laugh.

"Wow, Ma! That Mexican sun looks good on you." LJ posted with a heart emoji. Throughout the day, I get tons of comments and likes under my photos. I was shocked to see my mother even liked the pictures. Smiling, I head back towards the house to grab a coffee cup and see what's the plan for today.

After a full day of touring The Diablo Salvaje Distillery, I found myself even more intrigued. I was like a kid in a Candy store. Being this up close, and personal with the whole process from start to finish, rendered new respect and appreciation for the tequila business. I was so giddy to start the day, my body was practically vibrating. The first stop on tour was the agave fields on the estate. I learned that agave is essential for tequila making, and it takes approximately seven-eight years for agave plants to reach maturity. Looking out, I could see endless rows of agave plants that went on for miles. Señor Chavez explained that the Chavez family has been distilling tequila since the 1800s. He also shared that he and his wife started their own distillery when they were young, soon after they were married. I smiled to myself, thinking of Señor Chavez as a *"Diablo Salvaje"* in his youth. Remembering the story Gabriella told me. Seeing the love he, and his wife shares, I know her father had to eventually come around. They were adorable.

Before going inside the distillery, I was shown where the freshly harvested agave is cut into halves and put into a brick oven, where the thirty-six-hour roasting process begins. This is where the starch turns to sugar. Once we entered the distillery, my senses immediately came alive. With all the smells that wafted through the air. It kind of gave off a roasted sweet potato smell. And being someone that loves sweet potatoes, I was in heaven. I truly enjoyed the pieces of sweet roasted agave given along the tour. As soon as it touched my tongue, I closed my eyes, savoring the sweet taste. It is sweeter than sugar, which took me by surprise. It has more rich honey or molasses sweetness to it.

When it was time for the tequila tasting, I decided to join in at the last minute. I hurried over to the group that was waiting for the tasting to begin.

In a big, boisterous voice, Señor Chavez begins, "Did you know, it is best to use all five senses when tasting tequila?" He states, holding up his large palm while looking around with a smirk. "You want first to *smell* it," he says as he brings the glass to his nose, inhaling deeply. "Then you need to look at it, to *see* it." Holding the glass up to the light, he observes it with a critical eye. "You can also *touch* it," he says, pouring a little into his hand and rubbing it between large worn fingers. "And of course, you have to *taste* it." he chuckles deeply, with a knowing smirk. "To taste Diablo Salvaje tequila properly, you must first exhale the air out through your nose before drinking the tequila to taste its actual flavor." He demonstrated while we watched on in awe.

"And finally!" his voice booms, "Your fifth sense!" he turns to look at us with a large grin, lifting his glass, prompting us to do the same. "To *hear*, Salud! as well as all the laughter that's sure to follow because a good time is sure to be had by everyone!" He finishes letting out an infectious laugh. I look around to see everyone following suit, raising their glasses, and bellowing Salud! Before drinking their tequila. I did the same, without taking the shot, of course. I know some would ask, *"why would you even take a tour of a tequila distillery while pregnant?"* Well, to that, I say.. there was absolutely no way in hell I was going to allow this golden opportunity to slip through my fingers. I also wasn't going to have Señor Chavez regretting his decision to invite me here. So, I improvised. Later that night, after one of the best Mexican dinners I've ever eaten, I decided to turn in early to rest my tired body.

Rough, calloused hands so unlike my husband's, glide up my body... hot lips kissing down my back... strong hands, rolling me onto my back, opening my legs wide as he pleases me with his hand...

My eyes fly open as I sit straight up in bed. "What in the hell was that?" I say, panting. With my hand on my chest, I try to get my galloping heart under control.

The next morning, I woke to the warm sun hitting my face. With my eyes still closed, I smile as my mind replays the day before. I truly enjoyed every moment of the tour. Señor Chavez was an amazing tour guide. Learning about this distillery's rich history and culture made me appreciate tequila on more of a personal level. I can now appreciate each bottle I have sheltered at home. Señor Chavez is a beast of a man who spoke with so much passion as he explained the distillery's history and operation. You couldn't help becoming enthralled by it. I can't wait to share all of this with Gio and to thank him once again. This trip wouldn't have been possible if he hadn't spoken so kindly of me. Feeling myself begin to doze off again, I give my head a light shake and start thinking about the day. It's still pretty early, but by the intensity of these early morning rays, I know I need to prepare myself for another scorcher. Rolling onto my back, I yawn and have a long welcomed stretch.

My mind instantly goes back to that dream, or was it a flashback? This is the second time I've had this dream. It didn't feel like a normal dream. It felt much too real. Another thing that stood out about this dream, I didn't feel any fear of this dreamscape man. Almost as if he was familiar to me somehow.

Biting down on my lower lip, I spend a few more minutes trying to make sense of it all before giving my head a shake. "Ok, enough, Sam, " I chastise myself. I decided at that very moment to put all thoughts that didn't pertain to this amazing trip to the back of my mind. Slowly sitting up, I'm instantly hit with nausea. My hands fly up to cover my mouth as I jump out of bed, and run to the bathroom. I barely made it to the toilet, before emptying all the contents in my stomach. "Please, not today," I moan aloud, dragging my body over to the sink to brush my teeth, and wash my face. With a large huff, I brace my hands on the sink. Leaning forward, I take in my sad, and confused reflection. Unable to allow myself to be cloaked in denial any longer, I've finally accepted the fact that I'm pregnant and going to be a mama again. The last part almost made me smile, before I heard, *at your age.* Immediately looking down, I fight with myself to mentally cast out those negative thoughts. Slowly shaking my head, I say to the room, "They have no place here." Pulling my eyes back up to my reflection, I whisper, "come on, Sam, you can do this, girl. You can have everything you've ever wanted." Feeling stronger, I take a cleansing breath and pull my shoulders back. I pushed the remaining negative and unproductive thoughts out of my head as I turned and headed over to the shower.

CHAPTER THIRTY-ONE

Sam

"Ma, where you at?" I hear LJ call from inside the house.

"I'm out back!" I yell back. Waking up feeling amazing this morning, I decided on Killa, and I was going to just have a chill day. I don't want to think about anything or anyone. I had such an amazing time in Mexico I wasn't ready to come down from my high just yet. After unpacking and doing laundry from my trip, I finished up a few things around the house that had been neglected. I put dinner on, grabbed Killa, and spent the afternoon in the pool. As I'm floating in the middle of the pool, I look over at Killa. He's floating away on his miniature float, with his shades on and all. Laughing, I rest my head back and close my eyes. I can't think of the last time I did this.

"Woah, mama! Is everything ok?" my son asks, taking in the whole backyard pool vibe.

I gave him a big smile before answering, "yes, sweetie. I just thought I would hang out in the pool today. Everything ok?"

Instantly, his handsome face splits into a smile. Rubbing his hands together, he says, "look at you, fresh from Mexico, all tanned up, rocking your Beyoncé braids. Just chilling in the swimming pool, like the goddess you are."

"Boy, you crazy," I say, chuckling.

"I love to see this, Ma. You, out here in your bathing suit, just enjoying yourself. You are amazing, and I hope you're beginning to realize that." He finishes with merriment dancing in his beautiful brown eyes.

Smiling up at my son, I asked if he wanted to join us.

He instantly sobers, "Dad called. He wanted me to see if you're free for dinner this evening so that y'all can talk."

Now, why didn't Lance just call me himself? I think with frustration. I smiled up at my son before telling him I would give Lance a call when I got back inside.

CHAPTER THIRTY-TWO

Sam

"Where in the hell have you been? Why do you look so tanned, Samantha?" Lance asks as I walk up to the table. Ignoring his questions, I take a seat across from him. We agreed to meet up at a restaurant near the house.

I look across at my cheating husband, wondering just how long he's been cheating on me? And, how many women have there been over the years? Lance has always been on me about my weight. Why would he even bother if he's been cheating all along? I used to be so afraid he would leave me for someone younger, prettier, or in better shape. A question that now plagues me is why did he stay this long?

'Look, Sam, I don't want to argue with you," he begins.

'I agree," I softly say, leaning forward as I toss my French braids over one shoulder. I give him my undivided attention, and I wait for him to continue.

"I think we should get a divorce, and before you start with all the theatrics," he says, holding up his hands, as if to stop my protest, "I just think we..."

"I agree. How do you want to proceed?" I interrupt him, picking up my iced water and taking a sip. I lick the few drops of water from my lips as I wait for him to proceed.

"Wow, Samantha, you've changed." He says, leaning back in his chair, staring at me as if I've just grown two heads. "Clearly, you are not who I thought you were."

Listening to him try to play victim rubbed me the wrong way. What I'm not going to do is sit here and allow him to talk down to me, when he's the one in the wrong. "Let's not do this, Lance," I raise my hands to stop his nonsense. "Like you've been a faithful husband," I laugh, "oh, and by the way, how long have you been having an affair with Cassie, Lance?" I calmly ask, staring directly into his eyes while a smile plays on my lips.

His eyes grew to the size of golf balls. His surprise rendered him utterly speechless. It really would have been comical if not for the severity of the situation.

He recovered quickly as he began to laugh while rubbing his jaw. "It really doesn't matter what I'm doing and who I'm doing it with, *wife*. You're the one sitting here pregnant with another man's baby." He says, pointing at my rounded belly. "And you can miss me with that sorry ass excuse that you don't know how you got pregnant or who the father is." He laughs as if he's just heard the funniest joke.

As I look across at my gorgeous husband, a deep sadness takes hold of me. "You know what, Lance, I've always felt that I was never thin enough or pretty enough or even good enough for you. I always wondered what you could possibly see in me; clearly, you could have had any woman you wanted." I paused to collect my thoughts before I continued. "As I got older, the fear of losing you made me desperate. Sitting here, I realize this is on me, not you."

Before he could make a smug reply, I continued.

"I gave you entirely way too much power and control over

my happiness. That stops now." Realizing this conversation, like our marriage was over, I stand to leave.

Before leaving, I place the tip of my clutch on the table and look down at him. "You were once one of my best friends. When we get to the bottom of this, because we will, you're going to regret how poorly you treated me. I may be a lot of things, but you know I have never been a liar. Goodbye, Lance."

As I made my way to the door, I glanced back in time to see a look of uncertainty cross his face. Maybe, he finally realized I might be telling the truth. Either way, it's too late.

Driving home, I think about my mother. I know a lot of my deepest-rooted insecurities are due to her constantly commenting on my weight. Always putting me on diets. I guess she believed men only wanted a certain type of woman, and knowing one of her daughters didn't fit that description plagued her. I'm beginning to understand. She thought she was helping me, thinking I wouldn't be able to find a man to love me unless I was slim. My grandma Hattie never had that problem. Even in her older years, she had a shape that had men half her age staring after her. Laughing out loud, I remember one time when my sisters and I were walking with grandma Hattie through the swap meets in LA. I would see men doing double takes when she walked by. I remember her saying, "Samantha, baby, you need to embrace those curves grandma Hattie gave you," chuckling at her comment as she walked into the kitchen. A smile pulls at my lips, thinking about my beloved grandmother. Maybe she was right. Maybe it's time for me to accept Sam as she is.

CHAPTER THIRTY-THREE

Gio

"It's been a minute, man. What's been up with you?" Lance asks, taking a sip of his drink. We're sitting at a table in one of our favorite sports bars.

I look across at a man that has been my best friend for over half my life. Taking a sip of my drink, I smile before speaking. "You know exactly where I've been. Taking care of GLS, just trying to hold everything down while you've been...out" I finish letting some of my annoyance come through.

"Come on, man, don't tell me you're salty about me taking a few "personal days," he air-quotes before continuing. You already know what went down with Sam, right? I just needed a break from all that. To take a step back to assess everything. You know, see what I wanted to do, what direction I wanted to take." He finishes with a smug smile, bringing his glass to his lips.

"Yeah, I've heard," I say with a raised eyebrow while sipping my own rum and coke.

"Look, Lance, you and I have been friends for a long time, and you know I'm not one to beat around the bush, simply put, I want Sam. I've wanted her from the very beginning. Something you were very much aware of." I say pointedly.

"Hey man, look, it wasn't my fault you were too chicken shit to do anything about it." He says with his hands up.

"So what, you think this is your time now. You're going to swoop in and save the day or some shit." He says, laughing. Instantly, he becomes serious, slamming his palms down on the table, almost spilling his drink. "That's my wife!" He hisses.

Unfazed by his outburst, I calmly replied. "That you recently asked for a divorce, right? That wife?"

We stare at each other for a while before a smile splits his face. "Shit," he says, leaning back, folding his arms over his chest. "It's probably you she's been fucking all this time. Tell me, Gio, is my wife carrying your baby?"

Not losing my cool, I take another sip of my drink before saying. "Unlike you, my friend, I've never forgotten the remarkable woman that is Samantha Lane. I know she's loyal to a fault and, most importantly, honest. I believe something unspeakable has happened to her, and I plan to be by her side and help her through this."

With all of his cool composure gone. He yells, "You called it right, mother fucker! Samantha Lane is my wife! She has my last name!" He emphasizes this by slapping his chest.

Gio stands up, buttoning his coat while saying, "Whatever the case, I must thank you. You've cleared my way to something I've wanted for a very long time. I really do feel sorry for you, old friend. When you come to your senses and realize all those women you sleep around with were never half the woman Sam is combined... hmm." I paused, deciding it was best to let my words sink in and let him draw his own conclusions."

"Be well, old friend," I say before heading towards the door.

CHAPTER THIRTY-FOUR

Sam

I'm sitting in front of my vanity, putting the finishing touches on my hair and makeup, when I hear the doorbell ring. I leaned back to glance at the clock before smiling. "Eight PM. on the dot," I say out loud. I took my time getting dressed this evening. The plan was to seduce. Or at least attempt a seduction. I laugh to myself. Opening the door, Gio's standing there, looking sexy as hell holding the most beautiful roses. *Lord, this man is fine*, I think to myself, biting my lip.

"For you, beautiful," he says, stepping inside.

I took the flowers, inhaling the beautiful fragrance, before placing them on the table so that I could thank him properly.

"You're always so thoughtful, Giovanni. Thank you." Going up on my toes, I placed a kiss on his lips. Before I could back away, strong arms are pulling me close as he takes my small kiss to the next level. One large hand holds me close as the other begins to softly caress the back of my neck, sending chills down my spine.

Moaning softly, I reach up to bury my hands in his silky hair.

Not breaking our kiss, he walks us further inside and closes the door with his foot. Finally coming up for air, I look into his eyes and tell him what I've been feeling for so long.

"I love you, Gio."

"Oh, yeah?" He says, holding on to me tighter as his gaze grows hungry.

"I need to hear you say it again, Mia Bella. I've wanted to hear those words uttered from those beautiful lips for so long. Please say them again." He whispers against my lips.

I couldn't help feeling like a giddy school girl. I threw my head back, laughing, and yelled, "I love you, Giovanni Michelangelo Rossi!"

After dinner, we snuggle up on the couch to watch a movie.

"Come on, Mia Bella, let's get you to bed," Giovanni whispers in my ear.

Slowly opening my eyes, I look around, trying to orient myself. I see the tv is now turned off and realize I must have fallen asleep.

Laughing, I ask. "Well, was the movie any good?"

"I'm not quite sure, I couldn't hear what they were saying over your snoring." He finishes by giving me a devilish smile.

"Giovanni! I do not snore!"

I got to my feet, grabbed the blanket off the couch, and started folding it. "Why don't you go on and stay the night? It's late, and I promise to be on my best behavior," I say with a wink.

He stands and comes close before saying, "Now, why would you want to make a senseless promise like that. If I'm going to stay the night, I'm going to need you at your worst. He takes the blanket from my hands and tosses it on the couch.

"Come, Mia Bella. "He says, grabbing my hand and leading me upstairs.

Once we're in my bedroom, he wraps his arms around me and pulls me in close.

I don't know how long we stand like that. Taking comfort in

each other's embrace. Inhaling his wonderful cologne, I hear him softly say, "I know how self-conscious you've always been about your body. It wasn't my place to speak on such things because you belonged to another, but now that you are mine, I can finally tell you how your sexy curves have always driven me crazy." He grabs my ass to emphasize his point.

"Do you understand I won't be able to keep my hands off of you? I hope you won't get too upset with me. " He says, with a sexy predatory smile.

I feel shivers run down my spine as he continues to speak. "So you think you're ready for me, huh?

Biting my lower lip, I smile while nodding my head.

"No, no, there will be none of that tonight, Samantha. I need your words because I'm going to tell you in great detail what I'm going to do to this delectable body of yours."

He turns away from me and walks toward the bed. Silently, he removes his shirt and tie, tossing them onto the side chair. *"God, this man is beautiful."* I thought to myself as I took him in. Facing me, he removes his pants, keeping on his boxers. My eyes track his every move as he sits on the edge of the bed. Slowly he leans forward, with his elbows now resting on his knees.

"I know it's going to take some time for you to feel completely comfortable being naked in front of me, but I plan to help you with that starting tonight, Mia Bella."

"Now strip."

Taken by surprise, I stand there staring at him in shock. I can't do this. I think as all my insecurities assault my mind at once.

"Samantha!" Gio's deep voice cuts through my thoughts. "Get out of that beautiful head of yours, and do as I asked. You're one of the sexiest women I know. Please don't make me wait. I'm dying to see those luscious curves, Mia Bella. Relax and just focus on me."

I don't know how long I stood there before throwing caution to the wind and timidly doing as he asked. Once I untied my wrap dress and opened it, I was rewarded with a growl of approval. I let the dress slide from my body down to the floor. Knowing there would be no sexy way to remove my bra due to the sheer size of my breasts, I decided to get some assistance. Taking a few steps to him, I stand between his legs and unsteadily turn around. Answering my silent request, I feel warm hands on my back. He unhooked my bra, then slid the straps down, helping it fall to the floor. Before I could take a step forward, he leaned in placing a kiss on my lower back. Feeling goosebumps break out on my arms, I can't help the small shutter that moves through me. He places his hands on my wide hips and begins to pull my panties down. When they're around my ankles, he assists me with stepping out of them. He stands behind me, bringing his large hands up to capture my breasts. Breathing hard, I lean my head back against his shoulder as he begins to fondle and massage them.

"You don't know how long I've wanted to feel these luscious melons in my hands like this. How I've dreamed of sucking them all night long." He breathes into my ear.

"The torture I had to endure, Samantha." He says hotly against my neck while punishing my nipples, causing my knees to buckle and a soft cry to leave my lips.

"Let's see what other treasures await, shall we?" Sending his hand lower down my body, he slipped a long finger between my folds.

Widening my legs to give him better access to me, he begins to lightly rub my clit.

Once he begins to speak, my body starts to squirm in his embrace.

"Look how wet you are for me, Samantha. I'm going to lay you down and eat your pussy so good your eyes are going to roll to the back of your head. Would you like that, mi amore? Do you want to cum so hard your stomach cramps?"

He applied more pressure to my clit while squeezing my nipple, causing me to let out a shuddering breath as my body began to move on its own accord.

"Once I have you dripping wet and out of your mind with lust, I'm going to make love to you so good, you will think twice about ever keeping this lovely body from me ever again. How does that sound?" He asks, pinching my clit.

While moaning loudly, all I can do is nod.

"No, no, no, Samantha," He says, giving my clit three sharp slaps, causing pleasure to slice through me.

"I need your words. Let's try again. How does that sound?"

"Yes! Oh god, yes, Gio, please." I beg as he thrusts two fingers into my soaking pussy.

Tell me what you want, Sam. What do you want me to do first? Eat your pussy until you come all over my mouth? Or to fuck you, tell me now?"

"Eat my pussy Gio please!" I say, almost sobbing.

Instantly turning me around, he kisses me passionately. Caressing my face, he tells me to sit on the bed and spread my legs wide for him.

So drunk on lust, I didn't think twice to hesitate. Leaning back onto my hands for support, I slowly open my legs, smiling up at him.

"Oh, Mia Bella, you bring me to my knees."

I watch as he pushes down his boxers with anticipation. This is my first time seeing all of him, so I take my time taking him in. I've always known Gio had an amazing body; what I didn't know was that he was packing a monster. His dick was like the rest of him, big, and magnificent.

I reach out to touch it, and he instantly swats my hand away, causing me to glare up at him.

While laughing, he says, "you didn't ask for my cock first. I'm giving my woman what she asks."

Before I could respond, he dropped to his knees and buried his head in my pussy. I don't think I was equipped to handle the amount of pleasure he unleashed on me. I really don't. When he brought his hand into the mix, opening me wider to allow his tongue to reach deeper, I nearly lost my mind. Thrusting two fingers in my weeping pussy, while he wrapped his lips around my clit and sucked hard was all I could take.

"Oh, oh, Gio, baby, I'm coming, I'm coming so hard." I said roughly, grabbing his head with my right hand to hold him in place as I rode his face. Unable to take the intense pleasure another moment, I clumsily scooted back on the bed with quaking legs, trying to catch my breath.

"Where do you think you're going? I still have your second request to fulfill." Not giving me a moment's rest, he grabs one of my legs roughly behind the knee while pushing the other side with his other hand. Now seated between my legs, he leans in to place a gentle kiss on my lips before delivering a powerful thrust deep inside me. The sheer size of him filled me so completely that I orgasmed instantly, pulling him deeper.

"Shit Sam, you're pulling me to the bottom of you." Gio gritted out.

Gio made love to me so thoroughly that night we both passed out in the wee hours of the morning. I swear, I woke up a brand new woman with a brand new walk.

Gio

The next morning, while preparing breakfast for a still sleeping Sam, Gio looks down at Killa and begins a conversation.

"I want to make my intentions clear. I'm going to marry your mama. I know how protective you are of her. Just know, you have no worries."

I laugh when Killa tilts his small head to one side, clearly uninterested in anything other than a piece of bacon.

I carefully walked over to his food bowl as he danced around my feet, I chuckled while placing a few strips of bacon in his bowl. "I'm glad to know you approve and have no objections," I tell him, scratching the top of his head as he devours my bribe.

CHAPTER THIRTY-FIVE

Sam

After a wonderful weekend with Gio, I can't help but smile like a schoolgirl as I walk next door to visit Ms. Sadie. At her door, I always press the doorbell two times to make sure she hears it. Inside, I can hear her shuffling towards the door.

"Who is it?" A strong raspy voice came.

I can't help but smile, hearing her voice, "It's me, Ms. Sadie, Sam."

I instantly hear locks before the door swings open.

"Samantha, I was just thinking about you!" She says, pulling me into a fierce embrace.

I close the door before following her into the living room. "How have you been?" I ask.

"Pretty good," she answers, smiling warmly. "How about you, baby? how have you been?" She asks with a concerned expression. I don't know how this old lady knows, but she already knows my situation. Maybe not all of the details, but she knows enough, I think to myself, shaking my head and letting out a little chuckle.

"Better, Ms. Sadie," thank you for asking," I answer honestly.

"That's good to hear, dear, and if you ever need to talk, old Ms. Sadie is here to listen, and whatever words you utter are kept between us, you understand?" She asks as her warm weathered hands enclose mine.

Believing her, I smile and thank her.

We sat there and talked for a good forty-five minutes when she remembered something.

"Sam, I've been meaning to call you, but you know how forgetful I can be sometimes. I remembered what I wanted to tell you the other night when I was washing Harold's PG&E uniform. Even though my dear Harold has passed on, I still wash his uniforms twice a week, Wednesday and Saturday, as I've always done for over thirty years. It was my job to make sure my Harold had everything he needed for work." She says with pride pausing to reminisce. After a while, she clears her throat and continues.

"I guess old habits die hard." She says with a light chuckle. "Anyway, when I was taking the uniform out of the dryer, something occurred to me." She pauses as she recalls the memory with her finger on her lip. "That man at your security system on the side of your house had on a PG&E uniform. Your PG&E meter is clear on the other side of your house like mine, so what would PG&E be doing tinkering with your security on this side?" She finishes. "It may be nothing, dear. I don't want to alarm you. I just thought that was a bit strange. I was watering my plants on the window sill when I looked out and saw him there."

"When did you say this was? I asked in a surprisingly calm voice.

"Let's see, oh, sweetie, this was some weeks back, right around the time I called you over to pick up your birthday gifts."

Instantly feeling chills, I shocked myself by remaining calm.

It was the hardest thing to do because all I wanted to do was bolt out of there with this new information.

A while later, as we're walking towards the door, she says, "Ok, sweetie, don't stay away too long." She stops at the door and turns to me. "I need to know that you and this bundle of joy are happy and healthy, ok?" she finishes while rubbing my extended belly. She smiles up at me, reminding me of my grandma Hattie.

I can feel myself getting emotional, as I promised I wouldn't stay away too long and give her a big hug.

As I'm walking back home, I'm so deep in thought I don't see Shell's car until I look up to see it parked in my driveway. Walking up to her car, I see her head leaning against her steering wheel. As I tap the window, she turns to me with watery eyes.

I smile and motion for her to follow me into the house.

"I'm so sorry, Sam, I... I think I went into shock. I didn't want to believe my sister would do something like that. Something so like... "Her," she says in an anguished whisper. "I've worked my ass off for that girl." She continues, "To get us away from that toxic bullshit. I had to literally sell my soul to the devil... She put the back of her trembling hand to her mouth to stop herself from saying more.

I've never seen my friend so distraught. I go to her and pull her into my arms.

"I'm so sorry, Sam." She cries, "I can't believe I abandoned you while you were going through so much." She cries harder as she finishes.

"Shhh, it's ok, you're my sister. I forgive you. I know that was hard to hear about Cassie."

I try changing the subject by telling her all about my recent Mexico trip to the Diablo Salvaje distillery.

"I must say, Sam, you looked good down there, girl." She says, leaning back, eyeing me while taking a sip of her tea. "Even though I was mad at you at the time, that did not stop me from stalking your Instagram page." She says, laughing. "I was like, no, this bitch didn't go to Mexico without me. Down there looking all gorgeous with those long-ass braids cascading down your back. I was like, yes bitch! Lance, eat your heart out, you no good mother fucker!"

'Shell!" I say, cracking up.

"And you did it with your cute baby bump on full display for the world to see. I loved it! And you're welcome, by the way." She says, leaning over to tug on a few of my braids. "I told you a long time ago these braids would look good on you. I'm not gonna even lie, I was looking at your pictures mad, jealous, and happy for you at the same time." She finishes with that loud laugh of hers that cracks me up harder.

A while later, as we continue to catch up, she drops a bombshell on me. With her eyes cast down, she says, "I think I miss Rodney, Sam." Knowing Shell as well as I do, I know this is not the time for me to reply or ask questions. I know how difficult this is for my friend to admit her true feelings, especially feelings about a man. So I take a sip of my tea and wait for her to continue.

"I don't know what's happening with me. He left a damn card on my windshield a few weeks back asking if I missed him yet. Can you believe the nerve of him, girl?" She says with a chuckle, but I can see the sheen that glosses her eyes while she speaks.

"Maybe I should just call his ass to let him know I'm good. Hell, I'm better than good, so stop playing these childish games." Bastard, she says to herself under her breath.

"But are you really, Shell?" I ask softly.

"Look at me!" she says, getting to her feet, giving me a little twirl, channeling her inner Kenya Moore. "I am what I've always been, and what is that?" She asks, pointing a manicured fingernail at me.

I chuckle and say, "you're gone with the wind, fabulous, girl!"

"Exactly!" she says, pointing at me before she plops back down.

"Can I say one little thing, Shell?" I ask a bit hesitantly.

"Go ahead, girl," she says with a huff, folding her arms over her chest.

"I really like Rodney for you, Shell." She's rolling her eyes before I can even get the words out. Noticing she hasn't interrupted me yet, I continue.

"I've watched you guys together on those rare occasions you brought him around. He watches you like you're his everything, and that makes me so happy because I know he sees the same beautiful soul I see." I finish with a shaky voice.

"See, that's the thing, Sam. My upbringing has made me too hard, too jaded to even take time to see or appreciate that. It's hard for me to believe a man can really..." pauses and bites on her lower lip as if looking for the right words.

"Love you?" I finish for her, "Shell, I know you don't lack self-esteem because you have enough for the both of us." I laugh when she rolls her eyes at me. "But sweetie, you're going to have to let your guard down just a little. I truly believe Rodney is worth the risk." Sensing she's over us discussing her love life, I move on.

After telling her what Ms. Sadie said, we sit there quietly trying to process it all. Then, Shell looks over at me and says.

"I think I know someone that can help," grabbing her phone, she made a call. An hour later, my doorbell rings.

I open my front door to see one of the most beautiful women I've ever seen standing there. With my mouth wide open, she smiles and holds out her hand.

"Belinda Washington PI at your service, you must be Sam?"

Shaking the glamazon's hand, I'm met with a surprisingly firm shake. "Yes, please, come in." As this midnight beauty passes me, I can't help inhaling her amazing scent.

"Hey, Belinda!" I hear from behind me.

"This is my girl Sam, and she requires your expertise," she smirks.

After offering Belinda something to drink, I lead them back to the living room. As soon as we're seated, Belinda turns to me and asks,

"Are you having an affair or seeing someone?"

Her directness took me by surprise and left me speechless for a minute. Recovering quickly, I realized I hadn't had the chance to tell Shell about me and Gio.

Biting my lip, I say,

"Oh no, I'm not having an affair. I am… seeing someone." As I say the next part, my gaze slides to Shell to gauge her reaction.

"I'm dating Gio, an old friend."

I watch as Shell's eyes double in size.

"I knew it!" She lets out a hearty laugh. "Sobering a bit, she says, "I'm so happy he finally grew some balls and told you how he feels."

"You knew?! I was completely astounded by her revelation. "For how long? And why didn't you ever tell me, Shell? I'm a little hurt.

"And what would you have done with that information, Sam?" She asks, leaning back against the couch and eyeing me.

"I will tell you what you would have done, absolutely nothing. You would never cheat on Lance's sorry ass. All that would have come from you knowing, would have been misery for you and Gio because you would have started distancing yourself from him, which would have been tragic. Despite how he may feel about you, he's always had your best interests at heart. He just wanted you happy, Sam, and if that lowlife made you happy, he knew he had to learn to live with it." Pausing for a moment, I assumed she was finished until she started with, "And Lance's sorry ass."

"Ok, Shell, I get it."

"Good," more softly, she says, "you deserve this, Sam. Gio is a wonderful man, and I couldn't be happier for the both of you " she finishes with a wink.

"So, you don't think Gio may be your stalker" Belinda questions.

"No!" This comes from Shell and me at the same time.

"Okay…" Belinda says while eyeing us.

I cleared my throat, before telling her that Gio was out of town with Lance on business around that time, so that wasn't possible.

Accepting my answer, she goes on to ask me about all of the men in my life.

After talking to Belinda Washington for the past hour, I've come to realize she's a walking, talking, wet dream. At thirty-five years old, she stood about 5'8 with smooth dark brown skin. To top it off, she has a curvy body that just won't quit. She exuded confidence and elegance, and was a woman in complete control. She was rocking a bald head that only enhanced her beauty and allure.

Shell made me laugh when she said Belinda was every scorned wife's secret weapon. She was very expensive to hire but worth every penny. If Belinda Washington sets her sights on you, you may as well give up or pay up. She's cunning, calculating, and extremely smart.

After Belinda left, I had to ask Shell how the two of them met; that woman is truly amazing. Shell told me she sold her an office building in a secret location a few years back. They've been friends ever since. I liked her instantly, and I'm glad to have her on my team.

CHAPTER THIRTY-SIX

Sam

By the end of the week, not only did Belinda have access to all my neighbors' doorbell cameras, but had their footage as well. She was also able to retrieve the footage from my neighbors on either side of me. Having a connection at the police station gave her complete access to all the cameras along my street.

We're currently viewing footage from the day before my birthday party. We saw the man in the PG&E uniform Ms. Sadie was talking about. He was definitely tampering with my security system, but unfortunately, we weren't able to get a good look at the guy. Looking at footage from another doorbell cam, I gasp when we see a man walk right into my house later that night after my pool party. The video isn't the best quality, so we're not able to make out his face.

"Damn it," I say with frustration.

"Relax, mama, we have more footage to go through." Came Belinda's calming reply as she remained focused on the monitors.

"You're good, sir, but not that good," Belinda says, talking to the man on the screen.

As we continue to watch the mysterious man, Belinda points out he knows right when to angle his body to ensure no camera can catch his face.

As I continue to watch him, I can't help but notice he's very familiar with his surroundings. Ever since the dream in Mexico, I had this sinking feeling that I knew the person. It breaks my heart and makes me feel pain just thinking about it.

When Belinda pulled the last bit of footage from one of my neighbors' bird feeder cameras, I gasped as a clear shot of Cole's face could briefly be seen. It's not the best video, but I can definitely tell that it's Cole, even with that PG&E cap pulled down. We watch as he pulls some things from his pocket and attaches them to my security system.

"Sam, do you know who this is?" Belinda asked after noticing Shell, and I went quiet. I sit there looking into Cole's face in total disbelief. "What does this exactly mean?" I say under my breath, absently shaking my head. Feeling as though my hearing had faded out a bit and is now beginning to return. I vaguely hear myself asking no one, "Cole, Cole did this?" I whisper in disbelief as I continue to look at the screen. Soon, I can hear Shell begin to scream. "THAT NO-GOOD MOTHER FUCKER!"

"Calm down, Shell." I automatically say, feeling anything but calm myself.

"Naw, fuck that, Sam. It's shit like this I can't handle it. It's triggering for me!" I can feel her whole body vibrating, as I slump numbly against her. "What do you want to do? How do you want to handle this, Sam? You already know I'm down for whatever." She finishes looking at me with fire in the depths of her brown eyes.

With my mind bombarded with all this information, my hands start to shake as I feel myself beginning to shut down.

"Shell, how about we give her a minute to process everything, ok?" This comes from Belinda, in that calm, authoritative voice of hers. As I sit there trying to slow my racing heart, I feel Killa tugging at my dress. Looking down, I see him frantically doing the three twirls, letting me know he needs to go out now.

"Uh, I'll be right back. I need to take him out," I say, slowly getting to my feet. I couldn't help feeling relieved for this small reprieve as I walked on unsteady legs to the door.

"Sure, sure, take all the time you need." was Belinda's concerned reply.

Feeling numb, I head to the door and open it, only to realize I forgot his leash on the sofa table. As I turn to grab it, Killa uses this opportunity to nudge the door open a little wider with his body and darts out. After grabbing the leash, as quick as my shocked body will allow, I walk out to catch up to him. Knowing exactly where he's gone, on autopilot, I turn and head in the direction of his favorite spot to potty. So many things are running through my mind at once that it's hard to catch a single thought. As I'm approaching Killa, I see two squirrels chasing each other across the street. All of a sudden, two things happen at once. Killa notices the squirrels, and I notice the blue truck coming down the street. It all happens so fast that I don't have time to react. "Nooo!" I scream as Killa runs into the street. I close my eyes tight, not able to watch. Hearing the squeal of brakes, I pray the driver was able to stop in time.

Breathing in, I open my eyes. As I take in my baby boy's lifeless body, the weirdest thing begins to happen to me. I start to laugh and cry simultaneously; that's the only way I can describe it. "Ma'am" I laugh and cry, "I'm so sorry," I cry and laugh, "he came out of nowhere" ... laugh-cry. "Ma'am, are you alright?"

"MA'AM!!!" The murderer shouts. I do this cry-laugh thing until my whole body starts to shake. I vaguely notice my concerned neighbors coming out. "Sam, are you ok?" I hear Shell's concerned voice asking from behind. Looking into her worried eyes, I try to answer; I really do. Suddenly, I start to feel the oddest sensation, like I'm on one of those spinning rides at the carnival. Spinning slowly at first, everything is a blur as you speed past by the end. I give my head a shake trying to clear away the fog and increasing dizziness. No longer able to hear the worried voices, I stumble backward as my world goes black.

CHAPTER THIRTY-SEVEN

Act 3

Losing Killa set my soul ablaze. I can't just sit here and do nothing. I refuse to. I'm tired of the damn waiting game, I think while gritting my teeth. It has been two whole weeks, and I've been relentlessly trying to come up with a plan to get Cole. I want this man to pay dearly. I blame him for Killa's death. If I wasn't so devastated and distraught that day, I would have made sure Killa's leash was attached before opening the door. I want justice for him, too. I think hotly, feeling as if I could breathe fire.

I'll be damned if I allow that sick mother fucker to roam free and terrorize my child and me. Not going to happen, I think, releasing a humorless laugh, I still can't wrap my head around all of this.

He's been like a son to me! I think in disbelief. Why, why would he ever do something like this? Taking a couple of cleansing breaths, my mind wanders to LJ. I've decided it was best not to share any of this with him just yet. I know he's going to be furious with me for keeping him in the dark, but I know my son. I'm afraid he would do something stupid and throw his whole life away. I release a sigh as I say into the emptiness. "Mama's got this."

With my nail between my teeth, my mind wanders back to the blue-eyed man that's blown my world apart. Did he think we would run off into the sunset together or something? It's all just so crazy. Cole is a gorgeous man. He could have anyone. What would make him do something like this? What am I missing here? "Ugh," I say, tired of my mind going in circles. I close my eyes, breathing deeply, trying to center myself.

"How are you holding up?" Gio asks, kissing the nape of my neck before pulling me into his body.

"Just anxious and sad," I say softly.

He knows I'm thinking about my fur baby without me having to say it. Turning me into his arms, he holds me close.

"We're getting close, baby. Belinda's team has been following Cole around and gathering information on his whereabouts. We're going to get him, Sam. He will not get away with any of this." Gio says quietly into my ear.

Pulling me towards the front door, he says, "let's get out of here for a while and go for a ride."

"No, we can't, Gio!" I protest, stopping in my tracks.

"Sam, we both have our phones with us. Belinda or Shell will call with any updates or any new developments." He finishes softly.

"You can use a break, Sam, even if only for a little while; think of the little one." He says, rubbing my belly. Knowing he was right, I gave in, and I allowed him to lead me out the door.

"It's all going to work out, Sam. You have my word," Gio says, glancing back at me. Wanting to believe him, I just hope and pray it won't take too long.

CHAPTER THIRTY-EIGHT

Sam

"We have to get inside his house." Belinda calmly says, making us all stare at her as if she's grown three heads. "*Damn it, only she could pull off being a three-headed monster and still be drop-dead gorgeous,*" I think to myself with a laugh. Yep, I'm finally losing my mind at this point. We've been gathered in my living room for the past week trying to formulate our plan.

"We need to get in there to find something we can actually use." Walking back and forth in front of us, she continues. "Pictures, letters, laptops, or even memory cards," she says while counting these things off on her fingers. Stopping, she looks at us with her hands on her curvy hips. "Look, guys, I know this is risky. I know how this works. That's why I'm volunteering myself to do it." She finishes looking at me.

"This time, when you go to the police, Sam, you will have enough evidence to back up your claims. I'll make sure of it." She finishes with a knowing glint in her eyes. I don't know who hurt this woman, but I could tell she enjoys the chase just as much as bringing men to their knees. All of the no-good bastards in the world should do themselves a favor and try their best to stay off Belinda Washington's radar. I think to myself, shaking my head.

"Ok, I'm on board with that, But... I pause to take a shaky breath. "I will be the one going inside. Just tell me what I need to do." I finish staring at her.

Right at that moment, as I expected, Gio and Shell started protesting at the same time.

"No, absolutely not, Samantha. You're pregnant!" Gio says while shaking his head.

"Girl, you've lost your damn mind if you think I would ever let that shit happen." She finishes looking at me as if I've insulted her. "Bitch got me all the way fucked up. I hear her say under her breath as she stands and walks off.

I look at Belinda expectantly and wait for her input. She surprises me by saying, "however you want to do this, I've got your back, Sam. I must say, I would really prefer to be the one going inside, but it's your call. I will make sure you know exactly what to look for. I know you can do this, girl." She finishes, giving me the courage to believe I could.

See, you can't help but love this woman. "Thank you, Belinda," I say to her as she looks my way and winks.

A couple of hours later, we finally came up with a solid plan. Belinda just left to start putting everything into place. I can still hear Shell and Gio going back and forth in the kitchen on how this is the worst plan ever. I know they're both upset and worried, but just like they want to protect me, I'm determined to protect them. I don't want anyone else involved with going inside, just in case everything goes south. I'm ready... or so I thought...

CHAPTER THIRTY-NINE

Sam

Belinda and her team had been following Cole around the city for the past two weeks. She wanted to know his every move. "Did I say the girl was good? She has had my mind blown with just how good and thorough she is. From knowing his day-to-day schedule to any changes in his routine. She had eyes on him from the time he left the house until the time he returned to it. She doesn't like to leave anything to chance.

As we're sitting around the large table in Shell's beautiful conference room, our eyes are glued to the front of the room as Belinda goes over every detail of the plan.

"I think we should go in this Wednesday at 11AM." She starts to explain.

"Cole is usually gone by eight in the morning. He hardly ever returns home for anything. He's usually out of the house for about ten hours. He lives alone, so there are no worries about a roommate. He doesn't have any pets. No dogs inside waiting to attack or cats for us to accidentally let out, alerting him that something is going on."

Pausing from the whiteboard, she turns to look at every one. Noticing Shell was looking down, she asks, "Shell, is everything alright? I see you're looking at your cell." She says dryly.

"Ah, just replying to a text. My apologies, please continue," Shell says, waving her hand towards the board.

Satisfied that she had everyone's attention again, she turned back to the board and finished going over the plan.

With furrowed brows, I glanced at Shell and mouthed, "who was that?"

She replied, "Rodney," before rolling her eyes. I don't know if she realized it, but I caught a glimpse of that small smile she had after mouthing his name. Giving her a quick thumbs-up, I turned back to listen to Belinda.

She goes on to tell us about neighbors and delivery personnel.

"Ok, Sam, " she turns to me, giving me her undivided attention. "Once you're inside, be mindful of your surroundings. If a door is closed when you first enter it, make sure it's closed when you leave out. We want to leave everything as it was. The last thing we want to do is alert him of anything just in case we need to go back a second time. Are you with me?" Once I nod, she continues. "You have only eleven minutes to be inside. So make them count. Make sure you hit the first places I told you about, ok?

She paused to make sure I understood this before saying. "Everyone else, set your Apple Watch to 8 minutes. Here you go, Sam," she says, handing me a stopwatch with a rope. "I would prefer that you have your stopwatch around your neck. This will allow you to keep track of your time with only a quick glance down at your chest. I want your hands free. I don't want anything accidentally dropping or being left behind. You got that?"

I gave her a quick nod and looked down at the stopwatch to see that it was set for eleven minutes. I do my best to avoid Shell and Gio's angry stares. They have been pleading with me to change my mind. Only after I threatened to exclude them from the whole operation did they finally relent. Sighing, I close my eyes while rubbing the bridge of my nose. We're getting closer. I can feel it. My nerves are shot just thinking about what I might just find inside Cole's home.

CHAPTER FORTY

Sam

Getting inside Cole's house wasn't as difficult as I thought. No wonder so many home robberies are committed in broad daylight. Definitely, a sobering thought. Giving my head a quick shake, I entered a large side window that was pretty easy to get through. Once inside, a weird feeling creeps up my spine. I do my best to shake it off, trying to summon the courage to get this done. Taking a few steps inside, I stand perfectly still and listen out for any sounds or movements. "Come on, Sam, let's get this done. You don't have much time." I whisper to myself. Shaking off the last of my fear, I quickly glance around, taking in the very masculine decor. I turn and head towards the staircase, quickly climbing them.

At the top, I see the bathroom at the end of the hall and two-bedroom doors opposite one another. The door on the left was closed, so I decided to go into the opened one first. Peeking inside the door, I can tell it's Cole's room right away as his scent hits me. Doing as Belinda instructed, I head over to the bed first. Getting on my knees, I look under to see if there's a laptop or any small storage boxes. Finding nothing, I slap the carpet with my hand, letting out an aggravated growl before coming up to my knees. I shuffle over to the nightstand and go through both drawers. Coming up empty, I quickly, well as quick as my pregnant belly would allow, get to my feet and hurry around the bed to check the other nightstand. Nothing. Blowing out a frustrated puff of air, I turn around and rush into the closet. Taking my small flashlight out of my back pocket to give me some light, I check around the floor for any hidden storage, then the top two shelves. "Damn it!" Breathing harder, I come out of the closet and look over towards the last piece of furniture in the room.

The first three dresser drawers held nothing but clothes. With my frustration mounting, I was about to close the fourth when I saw something small and black under a shirt. Pulling it out, I realize it's a memory card. I rummage a bit more before finally realizing that was it. "Well, at least it's something," I say to myself while closing the drawer. Back in the hall, I stop to listen out again. Glancing at my chest, I see I've only been here for seven minutes. With only four minutes left, I hurry across to the other bedroom. I slowly opened the door and gasped. A beautiful nursery was inside. It was decorated with everything a baby could need. As my unsteady legs take me closer to the crib, I see a photo on the beautiful nightstand that matches the crib perfectly. As I pick up the picture in my now quaking hands, tears fall from my eyes. I hadn't even noticed this picture of me was missing from my living room. Thinking back, I remember him looking at pictures the day I invited everyone over for lunch.

I feel my cell phone vibrate in my back pocket. I snatch it out and bring it to my ear with numb fingers. "Hello," I answered without even recognizing my voice.

"What are you doing inside my house, Samantha?"

"Oh, God," I freeze instantly, expecting him to jump out any second.

"Sam, you have to let me explain what you are looking at." He says a bit breathlessly as if he's on the move. 'Please stay there until I get there so that I can explain everything. I promise it's not what you think."

I realize he's not here, which prompts me to move. Tossing the picture on the rocking chair, I turn and hurry from the room.

"Careful!" I hear Cole yell into the phone as I quickly move down the stairs.

"Please, Sam!"

In my haste, I can barely register Cole pleading with me as I hurry down.

"Sam…" He calls before I cut him off.

"No, I have nothing to say to you, you sick bastard!" I scream. "You stay away from my baby and me!"

"I've got to get out of here," I murmur over and over again as I rush to the front door. Reaching for the doorknob, I hear Cole yell, "WAIT."

"Samantha, please stay there. We need to talk. If you go out that door, you're going to jail. Please, just wait for me. I'm almost there" He's breathing hard at this point.

Not heeding his warning, I yell, "Fuck you!" Before swiftly opening the front door, and ran straight into a cop.

CHAPTER FORTY-ONE

Sam

"Mrs. Lane." The judge speaks to me over tented fingertips." I would expect for someone your age to know better. You should be ashamed of yourself."

I instantly feel my cheeks heat up. The burning only intensifies because this reprimand was coming from an older black woman that reminds me of my grandmother Hattie. I'm beyond humiliated.

"And trying to keep this young man from knowing about his baby! Please tell me, what were you hoping to accomplish by breaking into his home?" She looks at me with shrewd eyes. "What if you would have put yourself in danger, Mrs. Lane? In turn, putting your unborn child in danger?" She finishes, waiting to hear what I have to say for myself.

What can I say? Never in a million years would I have thought things would have turned out this way. I don't want to tell her about my claims just yet. Something tells me now is not the time. So I just sit there while she continues to tear into me.

How could this spiral out of control so quickly, I think to myself.

To my surprise, she turns to Cole and asks if there is anything he wants to say.

I watched as he got to his feet. He straightens his suit jacket before proceeding. "Your honor," he says in his deep voice, "I don't blame Samantha. She's been under a lot of stress lately."

It took everything in me not to yell out, *"Because of you, mother fucker!"* So I just sat there with my mouth tightly shut. Biting my tongue until I tasted metal.

"All I want to do is make sure she and the baby are alright, your honor, and let her know I am here if ever she needs me. I believe she was a bit unsure of my intentions which is what led her to break into my home. I don't blame her or hold that against her. I hope you won't either, your honor. Thank you for allowing me to speak." He finishes before sitting back down.

"Am I in the twilight zone?" I want to turn and ask someone because all of this makes no sense. How did I end up being the bad guy in all of this? What we didn't know going in was that Cole recently had sensors and hidden cameras placed throughout his home. To alert him if someone was inside or around his property. *"Aww, look at baby daddy, wanting to keep his cub safe,"* I think with disgust. The day I was inside, he was alerted that someone was inside.

"Here's what you're going to do, Ms. Lane. You're re to inform Mr. Coleman Shaw of all doctor appointments pertaining to the baby from here on out."

I finally had enough, I tried to say, "your honor, that's ..!"

"Do I make myself clear, Mrs. Lane?!" She says, abruptly cutting me off.

Feeling hopeless and ashamed, all I could do was nod. Feeling defeated, I let out a hollow sigh. Now, what am I going to do?

CHAPTER FORTY-TWO

Sam

A week after that whole court fiasco, I'm relaxing in bed or rather trying to relax by thinking about my life. The old Sam would have just accepted all this as just being the story of my life and tried to make the best of it. I had become so used to living my life like that, living to please everyone but Samantha. Shaking my head, I think, "Not, not anymore." I'm tired. I can't live like that anymore. "Nope," I say out loud before taking a sip of my tea.

"Ma, you home?" I hear LJ yell from downstairs

"I'm up here, son."

I can hear him taking the stairs two at a time, so it took him no time to make it up here and walk through my door.

"Hey, sweetie... what's wrong?" I ask once I see his face.

He walks over to my side of the bed, gets to his knees, and silently lays his head on my lap. Feeling my baby's pain, I just rub his back and wait for him to let it out.

"Why do I keep failing you, Ma? I feel like you keep getting hurt when I'm supposed to be protecting you." He finishes as tears roll down the side of his face.

I take a calming breath before I begin. "Baby, I need you to listen to me. I mean really listen. can you do that for me?"

I feel him nod, and I continue, "I feel strong, LJ. For the first time in a long time, I feel strong." Pushing him back so that he can fully see the seriousness on my face, "I know a lot is going on right now, we're definitely in the middle of a storm, but baby, please believe me when I tell you, your mama is strong and ready to fight. We will get through this madness. So trust and believe, I'm going to be just fine. We're going to be just fine." I finish giving him a silly smile.

Sensing there's more on his mind, I wait for him to begin when he is ready.

"Ma, I talked to Cole the other day." I feel him go still as he waits for my reaction.

"What happened?" I asked, surprisingly calm.

"After I tried to kill him with my bare hands, the weirdest thing happened." He says with furrowed eyebrows.

"He… he didn't fight back, Ma. I think he would have let me beat him to death if I hadn't stopped when I did." Pausing once more, he looked off for a minute. "As I continued to beat his ass, something told me to stop. I knew if I killed that man, I would spend the rest of my life behind bars. Something I would gladly do to protect you, but then I thought, who would look after my mama?" He takes a moment to wipe his tears away with his shirt.

As he was looking down at his busted knuckles, he continued telling me what had happened. "I told him to get out of there, and I better not ever see his face again. Before he left, he said something that keeps playing over and over in my head Ma." He stops as disgust cloaks his face.

I take a deep breath to steady myself. I feel that what I'm

about to hear is going to give me nightmares. Only after mentally preparing myself do I ask,

"Go on, sweetie, what did he say?"

"He asked me if I remembered the story he told me about his sister a couple of years back."

"I was too angry and hurt to try and recall some story he told…" His words faltered before he said, "until I remembered."

LJ goes quiet, summoning the courage to continue.

"What happened to his sister, LJ? "Her name is Jasmine, right? I remember running into her a couple of times at the shop.

"Yes, it's Jasmine." He quietly says with a sad expression.

"After work one evening, I met up with the guys at the bar down the street from the shop. Sometimes, we went there to shoot some pool and have a couple of beers. After the other guys headed home, Cole and I sat at the bar to chop it up. I told him I'm close with all the guys, and I wanted to get to know him too. I asked why was he so serious all the time? I remember he looked at me for a minute before deciding to confide in me. He told me Jasmine was raped at thirteen years old."

"Oh, God!" I say as my hands fly up to cover my mouth, that poor girl.

"It was bad, Ma. She will never be able to have children." Sighing, he hangs his head as he finishes telling me. "Cole was only eighteen at the time. He said he tried to get justice for her, but with little resources and his sister so traumatized, unable to identify the guys, the case was dropped."

"After remembering that, the fight left me, Ma. I stood there and watched as he got to his feet and limped to the door. Before he walked out, he looked at me and said, *"I'm not reminding you of this to try to change anything, I just need you to know raping someone is something I could never do.* Then he turned and left."

What the hell is going on, Ma." He asks with eyes so torn.

I pulled him into my chest. I rocked my baby, trying to take away his pain. "I don't know, but your mama's sure as hell going to find out, I promise."

CHAPTER FORTY-THREE

Sam

My mind is all over the place this morning. I've been standing in my closet for the past twenty-five minutes, trying to find something to wear. With a frustrated huff, I walk over and snatch an emerald green maxi dress off the rack. Pulling it over my head, I take time to smooth it down as I run my hands over my growing belly. I swear I can't wait for all of this to be over so that I can finally take time to see how I really feel about this baby and becoming a mother again. Just thinking about how this pregnancy came to be, the whole Lance and Cassie drama, and losing my beloved fur baby. The last thought caused me to hesitate for a moment. Collecting myself, I release a big sigh. "I'm so sick of this shit!" Instantly mad, I refuse to be anyone's victim anymore. I refuse to live this life on anyone else's terms but my own. I do believe everything Cole said in court was true, but that's not my problem. I cannot have some crazy, unhinged man in my baby's life. That's not going to happen.

Thinking about Cole reminds me that I need to call Belinda

to see if she found anything we could use on that memory card. I know my son has my back, but he's also torn with what Cole reminded him about his sister. I know LJ's beginning to question if he could be guilty of committing such a vile crime. Well, I don't have that problem. He's definitely guilty in my book. I have a growing being in my tummy to prove it. I can also appreciate my son for trying to think about all this logically, without acting out first. Ultimately preventing him from doing something that could have potentially landed him in jail for the rest of his life. That is something I could not have handled. I gave my head a shake, not wanting my mind to even go there. Right when I'm about to make the call, my phone rings.

I glanced at the screen to see Shell's name flash.

"Hey, girl, I was just about to call you. What's up?

Not getting a reply, I say, "Hello, Shell, you there?"

"Hey Sam, Belinda thinks she found something that we can use. Are you home?"

"Yes, I'm at home. I don't have any plans until later this evening."

"Ok, we will be over shortly. Is LJ there?"

"No, he's at work. Why do you ask?"

"What about Gio? Is he there?"

With a huff, I snap. "No, Shell, I'm here alone. Why are you asking if they're here?"

"I just don't want them to see what Belinda has to show you."

I immediately feel a chill run down my back, softening my tone, I say. "No, no, it's fine. I'm here alone. They won't be stopping by until later on."

Twenty minutes later, Belinda Shell and I are sitting in my room as Belinda works on her laptop. Pausing, she turns to look at me.

"Samantha, I want to apologize to you. I keep beating myself up because I let you down. I should have insisted on going inside. Cole has probes monitoring his home that were strategically placed and were undetectable. I would never have suspected the level of security he has in his home. If he had put that in place himself, it makes me wonder where he could have possibly learned how to install something so sophisticated. With a setup like that, I wouldn't be surprised if he was on to us from the very beginning. At any rate, I failed you. All that I ask is that you allow me to make this right. I will get you justice Sam." She finishes looking at me with sad eyes.

"Belinda, you believed in me, girl," I tell her looking directly into her eyes. "You didn't make me feel weak or tried talking me out of going inside. You empowered me, I believe all I needed was for someone to believe in me, and you did. You gave me courage when I needed it most because I was scared shitless. I finally didn't feel like a pushover, or someone's victim, sitting back and letting everyone else take all the risks. So thank you for that. I don't blame you for anything. If anything, I need you to teach me how to become a badass bitch like you." I finish giving her a sly smile.

"Consider it done. Once you drop that baby, we will begin." She says, throwing me one of her winks before turning back to the screen.

"Ok, Sam, I'm going to take you through the first file, ok?"

I can't help but notice she's started handling me with kid gloves. As she turns the laptop towards me, I gasp. There are what looks like hundreds of pictures of me—going to the doctors, hanging out with Shell, having dinner with Gio. This man has been following me everywhere for months!

"Wow! I think we got him." I tell them excitedly, clapping my hands. Instantly, I notice I'm the only one excited about this. "What's wrong?" I ask, taking in how quiet they are for the first time.

"Sam, there's more," Belinda says before pressing play on a video.

I watch the screen as a video begins to play. I'm watching

what looks to be two people having sex. Cocking my head to the side, I continue to watch. It only takes a second to realize the man is Lance.

All I can see is his back as he's clearly having sex with someone that isn't me. Feeling like I'm about to throw up, I force myself to continue watching. As I take in the surroundings, my hand flies to my mouth. "Oh, my god! Is that man really having sex with another woman in our home? In our bed?" As the sheet slides from his body, the woman wraps her long slender legs around his waist. That's when I see the large black panther tattoo on the length of the woman's lower leg... Cassie. I realize with a sinking heart.

"I'm so sorry, Sam." I hear Shell say from behind me.

I glance back at her, and she has her head cast down, not meeting my eyes.

Even though I'm barely keeping it together, I can't stand to see my friend like this. Leaning over, I grab her hand, "Shell, look at me." Once she brings her watery eyes up to meet mine, I tell her, "this is not your fault. Do you hear me? Lance and Cassie are grown, this is on them, and I will deal with that. But right now, I have to deal with this Cole situation." A bit softer, I say, "I don't blame you, and you shouldn't blame yourself. Cassie is a grown woman." She finally squeezes my hand back. I take a cleansing breath before turning back to the screen.

Deciding I've had enough of literally seeing Lance's cheating ass, I tell Belinda to fast forward.

Right before she's about to do as I asked, I yell, "Wait!" Looking up at the ceiling and then the bed, I ask, "Belinda, is there a camera up there? How was this video even taken?

"I promise I will answer all of your questions, I want you to finish watching everything first. Is that ok?" she asks, throwing me a concerned glance.

I nod my head for her to proceed.

"Ok, Sam, this is the part you really need to see." She presses play as my hands fly to my mouth. I see Cole staring down at my sleeping form while he strokes my cheek. "Oh my god, how the hell is he recording this?" I whisper, leaning forward. I watch as he places a kiss on my cheek before whispering something in my ear. I'm not sure if I'm awake or not, but what I definitely know is I don't remember any of this. I continue watching as Cole stands up and begins removing his clothes. He briefly stares up at the ceiling, into a camera, I assume. He pegs me with his piercing blue eyes. "What the hell!" I say, turning to look up at my ceiling once again. I try locating where the camera could be hidden. Looking up, all I see is my ceiling fan and recessed lighting. Giving up, I turn back to the screen and freeze. He's still staring into the camera, staring right at me.

"What the fuck do you think you're doing, you bastard?" I say to him under my breath as I stare right back at him.

Numbly, I watch as Cole slides the sheet from my body. He looks down almost lovingly before lying next to me. Noticing I didn't stir once, confirming my suspicion that I had drunk way too much tequila that night. But what I don't understand is why can't I remember any of this? I've never blacked out drunk before or have absolutely no memory of what happened the night before. I'm shaking my head. I watch as he takes one of my large breasts in his hand and momentarily looks at the camera before taking my nipple into his mouth. With my mouth wide open, I watch as my semiconscious form lets out a sigh as he brings his right hand up to caress my other breast. He releases one nipple before sucking the other inside his mouth. I watch myself begin to moan as I absently cradle his head to my breast. My stomach drops as he leaves my breasts, heading lower down my body. Covering my mouth, I closed my eyes and just breathed. I don't know how long I had them closed because when I finally opened them, I noticed he was climbing his way back up my body.

After releasing a sigh, I say. "Stop it, please."

``Ladies, I love and appreciate you dearly, but I have to watch this alone." Taking a second, I swallow loudly before continuing.

"I just don't want you to see me like this." I finish, barely able to meet their eyes.

"We understand, Sam, and you have nothing to be ashamed about," Shell says, giving me a knowing stare. I'm once again reminded that my strong friend has been through some things.

After they leave the room, with a heavy sigh, I reluctantly turn back around and press play. To finish watching my humiliation play out alone.

I watch as Cole's large body is nestled between my legs. Holding my knees up, looking down, I assume to align himself to my opening. He slowly eases into me. I watch myself let out a contented sigh as I open my eyes smiling up into his eyes. Cole then leans down, whispering something into my ear as he gently moves inside me. Unable to watch anymore, I slam the laptop closed. My mind is having the damnedest time processing what it's seeing. Because I have no recollection of any of this, I feel that I should.

"Sam... Sam, can you hear me?" I hear and feel someone patting me on the shoulder.

I blink a couple of times while looking into Belinda's beautiful mahogany eyes. Giving me a sad smile, she asks, "are you still with me."

Nodding my head, she says, "Good."

"After looking at this footage, it had to have come from a camera in that direction." She says, pointing to one of the recessed lighting. "Were you aware of the cameras in your room, Sam?"

"Yes, but none pointing in the direction of our bed. They point more in the direction of the hallway. " I was shocked.

"I figured that because yours is still installed." She says, pointing to the ones I'm aware of.

"Well, Cole definitely knew the one in the recessed lighting was there. It's not hard to believe he's the one that installed and removed them somehow."

Looking at her questionably, she continues.

"I've checked. They're no longer there." She says, looking at me.

'Oh my god, he must have been planning this for a long time." I say to myself.

"Well, the good news is, I think we got him," Belinda says with a smirk.

"I think we have enough evidence to put him in jail. I had someone look into his background. He's had a couple of run-ins with the law. He was arrested for hacking in his late teens. He also had an assault and battery charge some years back.

She grabbed her cell off the nightstand and headed to the door.

"I will be right back, ladies, I have to check on something with an acquaintance of mine.

"NO MORE!" I scream.

I looked into Shell's worried eyes and continued. "I cannot do this anymore, Shell. I refuse to just allow shit to just happen to me." I tell her brokenly. "I'm too much of an amazing person to live with a broken spirit." I pause a minute to collect myself before continuing. "Mark my words, I will rise and be victorious because if I continue to just allow myself to feel so unworthy, it's going to kill me. I see that now, and I'm not about to let that happen for no one. Not Cole, not Lance, or even my mother. I have way too much to offer, I have way too much life to live."

"Well, it's about damn time." I hear her say before being pulled into her warm embrace.

"I've always known you were strong, Sam. I've been waiting for you to realize it for yourself. You want to know how I knew?"

Not waiting for my reply, she continued, "because you kept me strong." Drawing in a shaky breath, she says, "a lot of bad things had happened to me when I was growing up that I have never shared with you. If I was a weaker person, I would have ended my life a long time ago." She says with a humorless laugh.

She sensed I was about to turn to comfort her, so she hugged me a little tighter, preventing it.

"When those dark memories are too much and threaten to finally pull me under, I think of you, Sam. You would lend me your strength without even knowing it. Now, let's go find Belinda, and see how we go about nailing Cole's ass to the wall."

Pulling me with her, we go do just that.

CHAPTER FORTY-FOUR

Sam

As we're sitting in the police station, cold dread grips me. I can't help thinking about how things went the last time I was here. Sitting next to my lawyer, I look over to watch her as she's typing away on her laptop. Belinda told me Lisa was the best, and I trust what she says wholeheartedly. Hit with deja vu, I do everything in my power to reduce the anxiety that's coursing through me. Looking around, everything looks the same. Right down to the absent-minded officer at the front desk. *"But this time WILL be different!"* I conceive while strengthening my resolve. Sensing my unease, Lisa momentarily stops typing and leans over to pat my leg. "Relax, Ms. Lane. I can guarantee this will be quick and easy this time around. I have everything I need right here to ensure that it does." She says, patting her briefcase. Giving me a quick wink, she turned back to her laptop. Her sneaky expression reminds me of Belinda. *I wonder if they're related?* I think to myself as I continue to watch her.

"Hello again, Ms. Lane. How can I help you today?"

I freeze instantly, hearing that voice.

Before I could reply, Lisa was on her feet. With a bright smile on her beautiful face, she says, "Well, good afternoon, officer Baldwin, I'm Lisa...

"I know exactly who you are, Ms. Booker," he huffs out while glaring at her. Not attempting to mask his irritation and disdain.

"Oh, come now, Tim, I'm not that bad." She says with a soft laugh. Leaning in, she tells him, "I haven't given you boys any problems in months; let's play nice." She finishes as the kind smile slips from her beautiful lips.

If I hadn't been watching her closely, I would have missed it. The subtle change in her demeanor. Gone was the smart and caring businesswoman who listened to me, with kind and compassionate eyes as I tearfully told her everything that's happened. In its place stood a no-nonsense attorney. By the way, the officer is currently staring daggers at her; he knows it too.

She turns to me with her smile back in place. "Come on, Sam. It's a good day for justice, don't you agree?"

'Yes... yes, it is." I reply, smiling back, getting to my feet.

"Well, then, let's go get you some." She finishes, leading the way.

RESOLUTION

Sam

As I stood outside of court, I looked up at the clear blue sky, closed my eyes, and breathed. I can't believe it's finally over. I realize with a heavy exhale. After all the evidence was turned in, on top of Lisa being a beast in the courtroom, Cole was arrested and charged with sexual misconduct, breaking and entering, as well as a few smaller charges. Ultimately, he will be going to prison for a very long time. For weeks, I've tried to wrap my head around how he could have done such a thing. I don't know if he has "mommy issues" or something more. From time to time, I do catch myself having brief flashbacks from that night. That's very disturbing. Not necessarily about Cole, but myself. I sometimes feel as if I'm missing something, and there's something more at play. All in all, I just pray he gets the help he needs. Rubbing my growing belly, I feel one of my daughters' strong kicks. Gio and I found out a couple of weeks ago that I have twin girls, to everyone's surprise. I think Gio was more excited than anyone. I laugh to myself, remembering how funny his reaction was when they told us.

"Samantha." I hear a man call from behind me.

I turn to see Lance strolling toward me. He has been present during the whole trial, to my surprise. With my head slightly tilted, I watch as he closes the distance between us. Looking down at me, he placed his hands in his suit pockets.

As I stared into his eyes, I could see all the torment that lay there.

Finally summoning the courage to speak, he says, "Now that this is over, do you think maybe we could…"

Looking into my eyes, I know he finally sees the resolve reflected in them that has given him pause. Watching sadness cloud his handsome face, I know he finally realizes what I've known for months now. Lance and Samantha are over. Leaning forward, he places a soft kiss on my cheek before whispering. "I'm sorry, Sam, more than you'll ever know." Watching him walk away, my heart goes out to him. I really did love that man. He knows he's lost a phenomenal woman, but there's not much I can do about that. He'll be alright. I smirk before turning to go find my man. I know I only have a minute before he sends out a search party and embarrasses me.

Everyone decided to meet up at the cheesecake factory to celebrate. Turning, I see an angry LJ charging toward me. "Here we go," I say under my breath.

"Ma! you can't do that. Just walk off without telling anybody." He says, throwing his hands up in the air.

"Boy, I just stepped out to get some air." Grabbing his arm, I say, "let's go celebrate Sonshine."

EPILOGUE

Sam

As I look down into the smiling faces of my little brown beauties, I can't help feeling pure joy. Curious crystal blue eyes, so like their father's peering up at me, makes me smile. I want to hate Cole, I really do, for what he did to me, but looking at my beautiful six-month-old identical twin daughters, I can't help but feel that they are my blessings. I'm not quite sure what he was hoping to accomplish with all this. I just pray he gets the help he needs and that he stays far away from me and my babies. If not, we will definitely have some problems. I'm not the same woman I was a year ago.

Along with being a new mommy, I've started a SOMME-LIER DE TEQUILA course. To learn everything I need to know about tequila. There are currently over one thousand brands of tequila on the market I'm determined to learn more about. I've been working closely with Señor Chavez and his wife. Having my very own tequila brand just might happen for this forty-six-year-old new mother, I think with a smile. But what really gets my heart pumping these days is my Thursday evening target practice at the gun range with Belinda. I'm nowhere near her level yet, but she vows to get me there. On those evenings, LJ comes over to babysit his sisters. He's so good with them. It brings tears to my eyes. I have to keep telling him that he doesn't have to do as much as he does. He's still so young, go off and enjoy his life. I swear, between him, Shell, and Gio, I hardly get any time with the girls. I chuckle to myself, as I think about their expressions when I told them I didn't want a baby shower. Shell's reaction caused me to laugh harder. *"See, this that shit I be talking about, Sam. You already know I'm not having any kids in this lifetime, so I have to live vicariously through you. And now you want to take this one little thing away from me. I'm hurt, Sam, I'm hurt."* *She finishes looking pitiful.*

I sober as my mind wanders to Lance. He's had the hardest time with all of this. Once the truth came out, he wanted Cole dead. He begged for me to take him back. Even suggested counseling which was huge for him. I let him know that our time had passed. I'm a different woman now but still wanted the best for him. He tried to apologize about the whole Cassie situation and how wrong he was for that. I held my hand to stop him and told him it wasn't necessary. It all worked out as it should have in the end. I'm far too happy to harbor any ill will towards him or Cassie. That doesn't mean I want either one of them in my life. It works for me if I never see either one again. I choose not to allow his betrayal to block my heart. Because of that, I have a wonderful man in my life. Of course, he wasn't too thrilled seeing me and Gio together. Gio can't seem to keep his hands off me, no matter where we're at or who's around. We've had a couple of awkward moments at GLS recently when Lance walked in, finding us in a steamy lip-lock. He's also caught me coming out of Gio's office adjusting my wrap dress. The look on his face was priceless. Clearing my throat, I told him Gio would be right with him before excusing myself and sashaying right into my office.

Leaving the girls' nursery, I head to my bedroom feeling so grateful for my life. My mother and I have never been close, and I don't think we ever will be, but we're trying to repair some parts of our relationship. I am doing it for my daughters. I will make sure they know how beautiful they are, no matter what size. The key is to value yourself first and foremost. Never changing that for anyone. Hearing the shower, I smile and hurry that way. Leaning against the door, I pull my lip between my teeth as I take in my gorgeous man. Standing in the shower with his back to me, I watch as the water cascades down his broad back and sculpted ass. Just standing here watching, a wicked thought crossed my mind. He's been so good lately, I think I will reward him with a little role play tonight, wearing that cute little outfit I picked up shopping with Shell. I noticed she picked one up for herself in another color. I didn't comment on it. I think she and Rodney have been working through some things. I'm so happy for my friend. She deserves love and happiness. Feeling raw lust slice through me as I continued watching Gio, I took off all of my clothes and joined him in the shower. Once inside, I'm instantly pulled into his arms.

"What took you so long, my love?" He says, nipping at my lower lip as he begins exploring my body with his slick hands. "Were my beautiful darlings giving their mother a hard time again?" He asks, causing me to giggle as he kisses down my neck.

"They're only "darling angels" when daddy puts them down for a nap. They give me hell, every chance they get. They really have you wrapped around their little fingers, Gio, you better be careful." I say with a chuckle, growing serious for a moment. "Thank you, baby. Thank you for loving me unconditionally." I say with a shaky voice, caressing his gorgeous face.

"You don't have to thank me, Mia Bella. All I ever wanted was for you to see the beauty in yourself that I've always seen in you from the very moment we met. You and the girls are my everything. My goal in life is to ensure they're happy, and that starts with me making their mommy happy. Now, no more talking. Let's enjoy this shower properly, shall we?"

"I can't think of anything better," I say, licking my lips while sliding to my knees.

SAN QUENTIN STATE PRISON

Cole

"Shaw! you have a visitor."

Cole raises his head off his cot and peers over at the guard, wondering if he made a mistake. He waits to hear his name called again before getting up. Who could possibly be coming to see him? His sister won't be here until Sunday. Jasmine has been the only person to visit him since he's been here, and that's fine with him. He really doesn't care to see anyone else, unless it's Samantha, of course, but he knows that's unlikely to ever happen. She stays on his mind constantly. Laying back with one arm behind his head, his thoughts once again drift to his beauty. His sister was able to find out that she had given birth to twin girls. Not able to keep the shit-eating grin off his face, he didn't try. He's so proud of that woman. If he had one wish, it would be to talk to her and explain why he did what he did and what really happened that night. No one knows the truth, and he will go to his grave with it. Samantha is the only person he would talk to about that. He knows that's never going to happen, and he's made peace with it. Just knowing he gave her something so special that she's always wanted will have to be enough. He's happy with the knowledge she will always have a piece of him.

As he's escorted down to the visiting bay, he's wondering who could be here to visit. Doubting it's anybody he cares to see, he just wants to get it over with so that he can go back to his cell. Commissary comes in today.

He walks through the doorway and stops in his tracks.

"Hello Cole," Lance says with a wide smile.

Shocked to see him here. "What the fuck are you doing here?" Cole asked as he walked further into the room, closing the distance.

"Come on now, is that how you're going to greet an old friend? Especially one you owe quite a bit of money to nonetheless."

"We are not friends, mother fucker, and I don't owe you shit!" I growl, wishing my hands weren't cuffed so that I could slam my fist into his smug face.

He continues to smile with a sinister gleam in his eyes. "Oh come now, Cole, why all the aggression?" he asks as if reading my mind.

"I paid you for a job you didn't complete, therefore, you owe me. Let's have a seat, so we can catch up," he says, gesturing to the table and chairs in the corner. "We have a lot to talk about.

The End

To find out what happens next and be notified for the release date of Betrayed by the L Word Book 2, sign up for my newsletter.

NOTE

To find out what happens next and be notified for the release date of Betrayed by the L Word Book 2, sign up for my newsletter.

AFTERWORD

I sincerely hope you enjoyed my debut novel Betrayed by the L word. If you enjoyed the book, I would appreciate an honest review. Reviews help so much! Thank you!

Betrayed by the L Word Book 2 will be coming out later this year. To get an immediate notification when the book is released please sign up for my mailing list!

ABOUT THE AUTHOR

Daphne Kane is an amazing mother and an emerging author from San Jose, California. She is an active and vibrant individual with a charming and enigmatic personality that helps her captivate and inspire everyone around her. Daphne is a certified nurse and has a vested interest in giving back to the community.

Daphne always had a knack for writing, and the drive to share her stories and make people's lives better inspired her to become an author. As an author of urban fiction, BWWM, women's fiction, and American romance novels, Daphne aspires to bring her reader the perfect blend of heart, heat, and humor. She always hopes to write stories that make her readers laugh, maybe cry, but always happier than when they started reading.

When Daphne is not working, she loves to spend time with her three sons. She loves her solitude. Her home is her heaven. She keeps the creative juices flowing by keeping herself busy with making artwork, sewing, decorating and dreaming up new stories.

Connect With Daphne Online:
www.daphnekanebooks.com